THE HOUR
BETWEEN
DOG
AND
WOLF

THE
SEAGULL
LIBRARY OF
GERMAN
LITERATURE

THE HOUR
BETWEEN
DOG
AND
WOLF

Silke
Scheuermann

TRANSLATED BY LUCY JONES

LONDON NEW YORK CALCUTTA

This publication has been supported by a grant from
the Goethe-Institut India

Seagull Books, 2022

Originally published as *Die Stunde zwischen Hund und
Wolf* by Silke Scheuermann © Schöffling & Co.
Verlagsbuchhandlung GmbH, Frankfurt am Main 2007

First published in English translation by Seagull Books, 2018

English translation © Lucy Jones, 2018

Published as part of the Seagull Library of German
Literature, 2022

ISBN 978 1 8030 9 004 7

British Library Cataloguing-in-Publication Data
A catalogue record for this book is available
from the British Library

Typeset by Seagull Books, Calcutta, India
Printed and bound by WordsWorth India, New Delhi, India

'The street was cool and full of grey shadows.
Lights were beginning to come on in the cafés.
It was the hour between dog and wolf, as they say.'

Jean Rhys, *After Leaving Mr Mackenzie*

I am nothing, no more than a faint outline on this morning in the narrow corridor between the swimming pool and glass facade of the building; a multiple reflection of a life that ended years ago, the shameless copy of many an opening sentence. I feel a cold draught through the chinks between the windowpanes that are stuck with bird silhouettes at regular intervals. The fat pool attendant, dressed in his usual white uniform, is sitting in his glass cabin at the other end of the hall. His satisfied face puts me in mind of a baker who has finished work for the day and is now sitting around, still in his work clothes. His attention is on his transistor radio; I can't hear the music he's chosen. Barefoot and in my wet, black swimsuit, I walk to the 50-metre pool and stand, ready to dive.

A minute earlier, I'd said goodbye to my sister. She had simply turned up here. I'd seen her coming out of the changing room as I was about to get into the water. I'd watched her very pale figure reflected in the glass walls; in fact, she was almost bluish under the long, neon strip lights on the ceiling. She had approached me and said hello while I had stepped aside to avoid her embrace, a defence that almost made her slip on the wet tiles. In any case, her hands had grasped at thin air, and she had swayed— but only for a moment—before regaining her poise. She's lithe, my beautiful sister; she's not the kind that easily falls flat on the floor in front of you.

The pool attendant had looked over, perhaps unsure whether I'd pushed her; I pulled a face, and he swiftly turned his head away again, to our left where the pool lay, still completely untouched, a smooth, blue surface. I'd followed his gaze: I would have gladly dived in at that very spot, rippling the water as little as possible, to swim my lengths one after the other until my thoughts switched off automatically. Ines had pointed to the Jacuzzi, her teeth chattering in exaggeration. Of course that was where she wanted to go: she'd always felt the cold easily, my big sister. Droplets of water glittered on her skin, and her wet hair was dark, almost brown. Long legs, an hourglass waist. What are you doing here? I'd asked, and she'd shrugged, Meeting you. I'd looked towards the glass cabin and thought that there was probably a baker somewhere in the world who would remind me of a pool attendant. Outside, beyond the glass facade, the grounds lay hidden in the winter darkness. At this time of year, everything lay idle: the pumped-dry pools, areas of trampled grass that were now supposed to recover, shapes stacked up on top of one another, covered with tarpaulin and hung with iron chains, chair sculptures, standing in isolation next to the trees. I knew this even though I couldn't make any of it out; it would be a good hour before it got light. It had started raining again; the raindrops, carried by the wind, struck the windowpanes and ran down in a steady, descending motion. It had been raining for days, days that began late and ended early. Outside it was bitterly cold and I moved from one artificially heated place to the next: the swimming pool, the newsroom, the library. If I couldn't sleep at night, I unpacked another moving box. I hadn't told Ines that I was moving back to Frankfurt from Rome. For reasons that I'd rather keep to myself, I hadn't been in touch with my sister for years. Being abroad had made it easy, and I preferred it that way; I felt good.

Four swimmers had passed us, their toned calves close enough to touch. I'd watched the first one glide into the water, had seen his skilful dive before he lapsed into an even stroke; the others followed. They swam their lanes and flip-turned, doing steady crawl movements; it looked beautiful, desirable of imitation. That's how I would swim too, very soon, when Ines left. I could already feel the cool, clear water on my skin. For now, I did little scissor movements with my legs, lifting my pelvis slightly, like some sort of weightless gymnastics. Ines said how she'd tracked me down: she'd read a feature I'd written for a Frankfurt newspaper and had guessed from the regional topic that I'd moved back here. She'd found out my address from directory enquiries, but had thought it would be more fun, as she put it, to try the swimming pool nearest my address early one morning. More fun, you thought? I'd asked, but she didn't elaborate, remarking instead, You stick to your old habits, don't you? Yes, I said, habits. My thoughts started to drift: I mentally went through my new colleagues. One was good-looking, always wore Armani suits. Armani, whereas everyone else turned up in jeans and sweaters.

Why did you leave Rome? Ines wanted to know; her tone suggested she'd already asked me and I hadn't replied. Well, I said, and scratched my collar-bone, German newspapers don't buy as many features as they used to. Fewer correspondents work for more newspapers, and here they gave me a good offer. As we were chatting, I noticed that there was sweat on her forehead; the warm, soupy air wasn't doing me any good either, perhaps because our conversation was getting more and more banal. We spoke about the pros and cons of Frankfurt compared to Rome: Frankfurt—who'd have thought—came off pretty badly. I stared at the countless stickers on the windows in the shape of black wings, which were supposed to stop birds flying into the glass facade of the swimming pool. They weren't the standard kind, I thought, no, they looked as if they were handmade, those strange big, black imaginary birds; I immediately suspected the pool attendant. Ines, meanwhile, had gone quiet, and I didn't help start up the conversation again. She trotted out a few more trivialities and then, after quarter of an hour, she said goodbye and left me in a bad mood. I watched her pull herself out of the water in her clingy, expensive swimsuit, black and wet like the world outside from which we were separated only by the glass wall of the swimming pool, and I thought: I am nothing, no more than a faint silhouette in the corridor between the Jacuzzi and this huge tiled pool. Then, finally, I swam.

She was sitting in the entrance hall, slumped down in one of the plastic chairs, with a red-and-blue sports bag on her lap. She wasn't wearing any make-up and her face was blotchy; she had tears in her eyes. It was the face that got her what she wanted: I knew it well, her bargaining face. I could hardly hear what she was saying but understood by watching the movement of her pale lips. She had a headache and asked if she could come over to mine for coffee. Of course, I said, returning her charming smile, or at least trying, because inside I was all churned up. How little things change, I thought, my sister's still up to her same old tricks. She had always taken advantage of her physical frailty to get whatever she wanted; in the past, she'd had nosebleeds at will if something didn't suit her, preferably at supper time when our father was among the audience. She seemed not to notice the dark drops falling onto the white bread in front of her, but Father, who always had his eyes on his favourite, grunted in shock and hurried to fetch her a flannel dipped in ice-cold water, which he'd press to the nape of her neck. When it was over, he'd twirl two pieces of tissue into plugs before inserting them into her nostrils. My bunny, he'd call her tenderly, and then the bunny would be placed on the green sofa in front of the television and would pick which film we would watch after the news. While this was going on, I'd be stuffing myself with leftovers from all four plates at the deserted table, only not touching Ines' bitten-off sandwich on which I thought I could see a drop of blood.

It had stopped raining outside; the air had a clear coolness to it, the kind you would want to seal in perfume bottles and spray around your flat; but in the swaying, rumbling tram, it was unpleasantly sticky. To the left and right, we bumped into dripping umbrellas. I let Ines get on first. She instantly tripped and knocked against a woman who had a dirty brown pram. Watch where you're going! scolded the woman, and my sister disappeared among the other passengers, her head ducked down. I lost sight of her for a minute or two in the anonymous crowd, and then spotted her again by the window of a four-seat bay, facing in the direction of the moving tram. Although the seat beside her was empty, a man with a hawk-like face was sitting opposite. His sly, over-familiar way of smiling was unpleasant; I didn't want to sit there. I waved to Ines and stood in the space near the doors. I watched her as we passed several stations, the way she sat there in her olive-green parka, her hands buried in her pockets; she looked frozen and seemed much smaller in this setting, just another pale individual on her unimportant journey through the city. I wondered what she wanted from me while making a sign that we should get off here, Textorstrasse. We walked past an old woman who had settled herself at the tram stop, surrounded by plastic bags stuffed to the brim and ripped at the sides; she gave us a slight nod. In her worn, grey-brown fur jacket, with startled, button-like eyes and hairs sprouting from her chin, she reminded me of a tired old rabbit.

In the hallway, the answerphone was flashing. Saturday, not yet ten in the morning—what a ridiculous time to call. So I knew straight away that it was for the American girl who'd lived here before me. I suggested to Ines that she could take a look around if she liked, as I was just going to listen to the machine, then expectantly pressed play. A certain Francis, familiar to me from dozens of messages, said that all he wanted was to be called back. He begged: Susan, please. Darling. I heard the note of desperation in his slightly nasal voice, noticed a new intensity and reckoned that things wouldn't turn out well for those two. Another regular caller, a woman who seemed to be a good friend of Susan's, had already let on that the couple had serious problems. But she had stopped calling; she must have Susan's new number. I took off my coat and rewound the pleasant voice on the tape: This is Frankfurt 615673. Please leave a message. I liked her voice and didn't want to change the greeting. Do you want coffee, Ines? I called and went into the living room where my sister was standing motionless in the centre of the room. She was staring through the glass door of the balcony with her hands now in the pockets of her frog-green hoodie, her hair still wet at the tips and tied into a ponytail. She gave off such a mood of inertia and dampness that it made me resolute, and so I marched past her, slid the glass door across and stepped out, my eyes automatically fixing on a spot on the stone floor. In the bright light coming from the living room, the small dark stain was clearly visible. A tiny sparrow had been lying there when I'd moved in, its wings spread, its head twisted to one side. Although it had obviously flown against the window, it looked as if it had been strangled, more a murder than a casualty. I'd put on neon-yellow rubber gloves and had slipped it into a rubbish bag that I'd taken down to the backyard straight away. I'd buried it in the paper container on top of newspaper reports about other casualties, and, as a small burial gift, I'd thrown in the yellow gloves. This went through my mind again, along with the decision that I'd made several times but kept forgetting, to buy some of those bird stickers like the ones I'd seen at the swimming pool. A blast of icy wind cuffed my ear. In the backyard, a plastic bag danced, rising and falling, twirling around as if on invisible strings. I pulled up the wide collar of my sweater even higher.

Ines, who of course didn't notice the blood stain—and why would she, it was very small—came to stand next to me, and we both leant on the balcony railings and looked down at the yard, gazing at the four bins and the row of atrophied tomato plants in silence for several minutes. After a while, Ines began to rock gently back and forth, her arms wrapped around her body, her lips violet-blue with cold. Sometimes, I said, two boys from the neighbourhood hang around here and play really strange games, torturing each other. I paused here, picking up on a small, intense sound, which turned out to be Ines' chattering teeth. And although out of politeness, she would have probably carried on inspecting this dismal view for a good while longer, I asked her in. While she sat down on a kitchen chair, rubbing her hands, I fetched the packet of coffee beans from the shelf. But then I remembered that our wet things still needed to be taken care of. Should I hang up your swimsuit to dry too? I asked. She immediately held out a wet bundle of material which I took between my fingertips. Soon our wet clothes were hanging next to each other on the bathroom radiator like dark phantoms, lifeless and clammy, while we sat, not much livelier, at the table with our cups. I'd made all sorts of noise while preparing the coffee and Ines had tried to make conversation; she'd told me about her new boyfriend, that she hadn't worked much recently, and only badly. I'd set down two large cups with biscuits and turned on the radio. They were already playing spring waltzes—now, in the middle of January. Even as I'd been putting out the cups, Ines had fallen silent and begun staring at the kitchen table. We went very quiet again. It was like flirting, each waiting for the other to make the first move and every little hesitation taken as a refusal to dance. I felt she could have made more effort, having forced herself on me this way, and I started to enthuse about Rome again, this time with suppressed anger in my voice. Ines stayed for about another twenty minutes and went to the toilet twice in that time. The last time, she came out carrying her still-wet swimsuit and speaking softly into her mobile; I heard her fluently reciting my address. While she was on the phone, I already fetched her parka, and, as I could tell from her aggrieved expression, she obviously didn't see my gesture as merely practical. This made me want to make it up to her straight away: I did so by saying how nice her parka was.

I hadn't expected her to give it to me on the spot. Come on, she said. No way, I said, and while we were still arguing, the doorbell rang. A man introduced himself as Kai and held out his hand which was almost as brown as mine; perhaps he too had been to the south recently. He was so tall that I had to look up at him; the frames of his glasses were almost transparent, and his eyes shone, greenish blue. I found him attractive even though he was Ines' boyfriend. I thought about what would happen if I said to Ines, He's good-looking. When Ines didn't come, I explained to Kai that she was sitting in the kitchen, and he briskly walked past me in the right direction. I followed him. How do you know which way to go? I asked. The old flats in this street all have the same layout, he replied. A friend of mine used to live in one. His tone was slightly disparaging, as if his friend and I, each in our own flats, were sad freaks in an identically laid-out world which we were not aware of. In the kitchen, Ines was slumped down. She greeted her boyfriend with lukewarm enthusiasm, a mumbled, monosyllabic *sothereyouare*, followed by Kai wanting to know straight away if we'd talked? About what? I asked and finally turned off the damned radio. No answer. Kai looked at Ines who was staring listlessly into her coffee cup. His gaze pierced the wet patch on the back of her hoodie made by the damp tips of her ponytail. My sister was hanging more than sitting on her chair. I'd never noticed before how passive sitting could be. Please, let's go, she said suddenly, taking her parka and leaving Kai to carry her sports bag. Feeling dull, my eyelids half-closed, I watched from the window as they walked over to a very old, dark-blue Mercedes that was parked across the street, the kind of car that advertising types and artists like to drive; it was quite possible that this Kai was a painter too. He didn't have his arm around her shoulders and they weren't holding hands either. And then it struck me that Ines was only wearing her pullover. Hesitantly, I went to the front door and opened it. Sure enough, lying on the mat was her carefully folded, olive-green parka. I picked it up and tried it on. It fitted perfectly. I walked around the living room in it a few times, and then, feeling too warm, went to stand on the balcony. The boys were there; the smaller one was wearing a cowboy hat and the bigger one, an Indian headdress. The Indian had strapped the cowboy to the rubbish container so expertly that when the boy wiggled, the whole container shook, and very soon he tired out and stood still. The bigger boy hit him repeatedly on the shins with a stick, always just on the shins. The bin jiggled a lot. I gazed down indifferently. The first time I'd seen the pair of them, I'd been horrified; Stop, for heaven's sake, stop, I'd yelled down into the yard, and they'd both burst out laughing and stuck out their pink tongues at me.

In the evening I was restless and roamed around the flat. I had just half-heartedly opened a moving box of papers—old letters, postcards, odds and ends that had once seemed important and that I'd always carted around with me, never looking at them again—when the telephone rang. Susan's voice brought the flat to life; I listened to it from where I was sitting cross-legged on the parquet floor. No one spoke on the tape; just a recurrent beeping sound could be heard. It didn't matter. I had just come across a tin that had once contained Danish butter biscuits but I now used to store photos, and this tin had my full attention. I fished out a pile with both hands and sifted through them quickly, like a picture flip-book. On top were pictures of Rome; underneath, older ones. I randomly picked out two from the bottom as if drawing lots: childhood photos, Ines and I on the beach. In the first picture we were standing side by side, laughing; we had haircuts with fringes and sun hats with checked patterns, and I, four years younger than my sister, was swinging a plastic bucket and spade. Our noses were sunburnt and our sun-bleached hair stuck out from beneath our hats. Ines was barefoot; I was wearing plastic sandals that you could leave on in the water. The second photo showed us playing. Only Ines' head was peeping out of the sand. I was busy digging. Ines was crowing with delight. I looked at this crowing-with-delight Ines and my younger self, digging and toiling away. With these pictures in my hand, shivering slightly as I hadn't turned on the heating yet, I sat there, remembering. She had loved this game and had trusted me unconditionally not to bury her head in the sand. She loved the feeling of the hot sand on her body, even rubbing it on purpose over her tummy and thighs. I never let her bury me because I was claustrophobic or distrustful. Probably it was just too hot for me. I stared at the photo: the sun, the dry heat, the trickling sand, white and powdery. On the reverse it said, *Oostende, Summer 19* . . . That was the year I learnt to swim; I had loved swimming from the word go. I traced the photo with my finger, slowly and gently, my eyes closed, and everything got bright, then brighter: I was lying on a beach towel, no, I was standing by the sea and looking out at child's height. I squinted at the horizon, moved my legs; water squirted and sand squelched through the gaps in my plastic sandals. Soon I'd be swimming. I wasn't wearing a bikini top because I didn't have any breasts. Ines didn't have any either, but she was wearing a bikini top as if some might grow while she was tanning herself, out of the blue; she'd always been an optimist, my big sister. When the phone rang again in the hallway, I jumped as if I'd been caught red-handed, put down the tin and ran to get it.

Kai apologized for calling so late. He seemed nervous and was smoking; I could hear a lighter clicking. He had to talk to me, he said. What about,

I wanted to know. I looked from the hallway to where he'd stood in the kitchen and imagined him now. He was tense, sitting bolt upright on a chair, a cigarette burning slowly in one hand. Not on the telephone, he said. Not on the telephone, that amused me. Where then? In a cafe? He agreed. Tomorrow would suit him, after work. Tomorrow is Sunday, I pointed out, and asked whether he was a painter. A photographer, he replied. He was doing a shoot. I suggested that I could drop by, and wrote the address on a Post-it. Then I stood in the room, unsure, the Post-it stuck to my index finger. Where to put it? I had stuck Post-its all over the flat as reminders; it was a quirk of mine. In the end I fixed it to the hallway mirror, next to the Post-its with the best hairdresser in town, or so I'd been told—a tip from a colleague in the newsroom—and the pizza service from whom I never ordered Italian dishes, only Vietnamese or Thai.

I set off early the next day, putting on my new parka, unpeeling the Post-it from the hallway mirror before going downstairs. Outside, seeing that I needed an umbrella, I ran back up to the first floor. Two blocks from my flat, there was a taxi rank where a lone cab was waiting as if for me. I read my Post-it aloud to the driver, who had rolled down the window to reveal his dark, monkey-like features, and then I sat in the back and looked out.

I'd never been to this part of town before, the old factory estates in the east, where the gaps between the buildings were empty and mysterious, and where enormous plots infested with weeds made superb playgrounds. I thought of the two boys in my yard; here they could pursue their torturous pleasures to their heart's content. Kai's old Mercedes stood in the lot between two other cars. I paid the taxi driver and walked over to the entrance, glancing up at the sky now and then; it looked like it was going to rain again. I nodded to the curvaceous redhead who was standing at the door for no obvious reason; I was about to squeeze past her when she assumed a knowing expression and said: You must be Ines' sister. Spitting image. I'm Carol. I'll take you inside.

A small group of young people dressed in black were standing in a circle around two tall, scantily clothed girls in summer dresses, perhaps fourteen or fifteen years old and leaning against the dilapidated walls of the warehouse in practised, lascivious poses. A photographer—not Kai, another man—was cavorting eagerly around them, kneeling down, propping himself against the wall, then moving back with his camera still trained on the girls. Do you want to watch? Carol asked. I shook my head slightly. She led me past the group and opened a black door, pressing the handle carefully before showing me into a separate room. The mood here could not have been

more different—it was dark and confined, and a con-
centrated silence reigned. Cautiously, I felt my way
forward along the wall for a better look. A very old
lady, in the pool of a white spotlight, was sitting in a
chair, her face so finely wrinkled that the lines almost
joined together to form an even surface. She had a
perfect, innocent, childish face, a face that was at
least a hundred years old, but you had the feeling you
could see eighty or ninety years into the past through
her skin to the little girl she had once been. I looked
at her slightly gnarled hands resting in her lap, which
reminded me of talons—the talons of a colossal,
mythical bird. An assistant dressed in black was
combing the elderly lady but she paid no attention
to what was happening around her; she just sat on
her chair in the spotlight, rendering the space about
her empty, a lonely island. I was so absorbed by the
sight that I flinched when Kai's voice suddenly spoke.
Let us know if the light's dazzling you, he said. She
nodded and moved her head to the left and right
when Kai gave her directions; otherwise a leaden
silence hung in the room, and no one moved—everyone seemed to sense the unnerving power, foreign-
ness and dignity of her elderliness. After a while,
which might have been ten minutes or half an hour,
the old lady's concentration started to wane and she
lifted her chin when she was supposed to lower it, or
confused left with right. We're nearly done, said Kai,
just this last roll of film.

I remembered an article I'd read about the oldest-ever laboratory mouse—the scientists had named it Yoda. It had lived to the equivalent of a hundred and thirty-six human years, more than twice the age of other mice. This was due to its leanness, reported the article, which was easy on the heart and circulation. However, it had always felt the cold; and for this reason, it had had to share its germfree cage with a roommate, a fat mouse that kept it warm all the time. I wondered what kind of life the old lady lived. Whether she sat in an overheated flat when she wasn't working as a model, and stared out of the window to see what was going on outside. I leant over to Carol and got a whiff of her strong perfume. She looks as if she's playing the idea of death, I whispered. Carol looked baffled. Sshhhh, someone hissed. What age had Yoda reached in mouse years? I couldn't remember; it hadn't sounded half as impressive. Four? When the lights went back on, I quickly left the room, Carol following me like a shadow. What are the photos of the old lady for? I asked. A public ad campaign, Carol answered. It's to make people aware that the eyewitnesses to German history are dying out. I nodded. So she's Jewish? Carol shrugged, like she was bored, and said, at any rate she's a model, a character model. Oh, I said and shifted from one foot to the other. Carol handed me a business card. At last, Kai came.

He wiped his hand across his forehead, glanced absently at my parka and apologized for making me wait. We walked over the gravel to the car. A young man wearing a dark leather jacket and shades with metallic-green lenses dashed past us; he waved, swung himself onto the saddle of his mountain bike which was leaning against the warehouse wall, and pedalled off at breakneck speed. Bye, Paul, Kai shouted after him. Compared with Paul, we dawdled to the car; in my hand, I turned over the ad-agency card that Carol had given me, wondering how Kai and my sister had met. I guessed at an opening of an art show. Kai unlocked the car door. Where did you meet anyway? I asked as I sat inside his extremely well-kempt albeit very old Mercedes, where some films and a bumper pack of tissues lay on the back seat. I waited for his reply while he put his gear into the boot according to some kind of system, and, although he hesitated for a conspicuously long time, I didn't feel awkward about asking. No, it wasn't indiscreet of me: couples always like to answer that one, it was important to the central myth. At a party, I think, said Kai indifferently, and started the engine. Ah, at a party, I repeated, but then let it drop. A party; he could mean an exhibition opening, of course. He would probably appreciate Ines' paintings, her radiant pastel-coloured pictures depicting happy people going for walks or reading on the beach, pictures that portrayed normal adults doing meaningless capers

or kissing each other. You could spot them immediately, these Ines Inah paintings; or I.I., as she was in
the habit of signing them. She used this alias because
our surname was very ordinary. Art critics were
bowled over by these distortions of reality. They
wrote that Ines rendered an inversion or an *ex nega-
tivo* of suffering; she displayed a brilliantly simulated
superficiality. In Rome, I'd talked to a critic who
wrote articles on the young art scenes in England,
France and Germany, and some other countries, I
forget where: he thought Ines' work was wonderful.
A newspaper photo of my sister at her first solo show
often came to my mind; she was wearing a velvet hat
that looked like a turban and a double necklace of
pearls. Her dress was creased on purpose, and her
hair slightly tousled, making her look like a thin,
expensive doll that someone had clothed in a hurry.
I had cut out the photo at the time—it was probably
in another biscuit tin somewhere—because, despite
everything, I was proud of her. It was not her pastel
paintings I objected to but those that depicted our
dying father in a hyper-realistic, frightening, indiscreet way—if you took into account that he was a
man who felt shame to the highest degree. But no
more talk of that. I asked Kai aggressively what he
wanted to talk about, my voice slicing through the
odious, family-daytrip atmosphere that had arisen
since we were taking a drive in the rain. Well, said
Kai, looking straight ahead, well, the thing is that

Ines would like to live with you for a while. Out of the question, I replied coolly.

We drove along the river. The rain changed, becoming harder, drumming louder. The other cars had now turned on their headlights and, as the storm unleashed itself, it was easy to forget that it was the middle of the day. Kai had long since turned on the windscreen wipers but they didn't help much; the rain came at a slight tilt from an uncertain direction, hitting the windscreen where the glass and hood joined, and spraying up to cover the window in gleaming streaks. I felt a bad mood brewing in me, a foul temper that matched the storm in a way I found idiotic and annoying. I tried to concentrate on a single, blurred raindrop but it didn't work and I felt humiliated—as if I'd fought with all my strength against a bucket of water, but lost. Kai had shifted into the right-hand lane. I could feel his eyes on me. She's not well, he said, and to top it all, there are building works outside her house and they're driving her crazy. She can't work any more and apart from that, I think she feels it's important to make up with you. My defences went up. Why make up? I asked. We haven't fallen out. Oh, come on, said Kai. A crabby tone had crept into his voice, a tone that annoyed me no end; after all, he was asking me for something, not the other way round. I studied my hand with affected boredom, my wrist, to be precise, on which I was wearing a thin, silver wristband. I pushed up the sleeves of my blouse and let my gaze slide up my arm. On the inner side I had small, white zigzag scars, I couldn't remember where from. I let my sleeve fall back down. Why doesn't she move in with a friend, or with you? I asked Kai, turning to face him abruptly, like an attacker ambushing her victim. This threw him completely and he sounded cagey when he spoke. My place is too small, and anyway, I have a friend living with me who has work to do in Frankfurt. Then she could move into her studio, I said, sticking to the same tack. It was a lousy excuse: Was his place too small or did he have someone living there? Kai, relieved to deflect the subject from his too small yet overcrowded flat, explained that Ines didn't have a studio right now. She had to leave the old one when the lease ran out and she's looking for a new one now, he said. Really? Now I was mystified. So it wasn't that she hadn't worked much recently and only badly, like she'd told me after swimming. She wasn't working at all. This was very untypical of my ambitious sister, not forgetting that she'd even managed to turn our father's death into some profitable business. So, how about it? Kai asked again. He was persistent, my sister's boyfriend, you had to give him that. I want to go home, I answered, please carry on driving.

I filled the kettle, still wearing the parka. As the water began to boil, I paced the hallway, then stopped in front of the coat-stand mirror to examine my pallid face, framed by my damp, bedraggled hair. It was a face that confirmed what Carol had said—that Ines and I were strikingly similar, too much so. I could still picture Kai's reproachful, crestfallen face and, as I took my first sip of tea, I started to struggle with my decision. I should have at least asked what problems Ines was having, even though I knew of course: she'd been running into these creative blocks since she was a teenager. Then she would latch on to someone—any Tom, Dick or Harry, completely at random—and suck out his energy like a vampire until that Tom, Dick or Harry lolled forward like a limp dishrag and Ines swanned back to her easel, perfectly revitalized. No doubt, I thought, grimly sipping my tea, no doubt Kai had already had this pleasure a few times and was now looking for some dummy to replace him. But I wasn't that gullible— definitely not. All the same, I made up my mind to meet Ines in the next few days, at least for coffee.

Evening came and I stood on the balcony in Ines' parka to smoke. I didn't look at the view. Instead, I thought of Rome: terracotta bricks and olive trees, the sun and chilled white wine served at the local corner bar. I realized that I hadn't thought of Rome for a long time. Strange: a few weeks elsewhere and the images of people and everyday places that were your life until recently start to fade. What if I'd met

Kai in Rome a few months ago, in a gallery or in front of the cinema? He wouldn't have known Ines; he'd have noticed me, I'd have given a casual wave. Perhaps he wouldn't have been able to speak the language, perhaps I'd have been able to translate for him as he ordered drinks or bought tickets. I threw my half-finished cigarette over the balcony. The backyard light went on. A woman in a dressing gown came out, pushed some old newspapers into the wrong container and went back in; as she did, probably noticing me because the light was on, she looked up and smiled. I caught her eye, saw her strikingly happy, confident expression, full of quiet contentment, and smiled back in imitation. Her trainers were loosely tied so that their laces dragged across the stones. I went to bed early that night. As I slowly undressed, I looked at the culture section of the newspaper. A new exhibition had opened at the Schirn gallery. I tore out the page and put it on my desk. On a Post-it I wrote: Phone Ines.

The newspaper clipping must have fallen on the floor, for I only found it two days later. My ballpoint pen had rolled off the desk, so I was on the floor, about to crawl under and retrieve it, and there it was. I looked up the museum's opening times online: Wednesday evenings until ten. I looked at the time. It was only eight.

I bought a ticket before remembering that recently, in a fit of frugality, I'd purchased a season ticket for various museums in the city. Leaving the cloakroom, where I'd been looking for some coins to put in the locker, I went back to the plump, neat lady in glasses at the ticket desk and explained my dilemma. She opened the cash drawer with little enthusiasm, took my ticket and gave me my money back. This seemed to upset her so much that I felt sorry for having asked. On the other hand, I now had plenty of coins. I stowed my things in the locker and went up the broad, curved flight of steps. Upstairs, I wandered about at random without paying attention to the layout of the exhibition, starting in the first room where I was drawn to a picture at the centre. It showed the head of a woman, the upper half veiled in black so that her mouth, which was neither beautiful nor ugly but simply functional, was the focus. I went right up to it, then took a step back, letting the strong colours and shapes work on me, flood through me. Once I'd looked at that picture for long enough, I walked on to look at another, this time a fragment of a head. Here the focus was the ears: they made the partial head look like some hybrid of a man and an ape. In the third exhibit, the emphasis was neither on the mouth nor ears, although both were recognizable; no, this time it was all about the eyes. I strolled on, stopped here and there, sometimes for a long time, sometimes only briefly, until an overall impression emerged of gashed lips, broken backs, twisted spines and legs that disappeared into nothingness. There was something hideously similar about all of these sitting, kneeling, always lonely men and women, making it hard to tell them apart. I walked around until I was tired and strangely chilly, even though the museum was well heated. All that time, I now realized, I had been clutching my season ticket so that it was now quite crumpled. A group on a guided tour came into the main hall and boxed me in when they headed straight for the painting in front of which I happened to be standing. But I didn't let them disturb me. Instead, I turned slightly and looked at each person in the same way in which I had looked at each painting: there was a woman with flashing teeth and golden hoop earrings almost down to her shoulders, who, despite being blonde, had a Latin flair to her movements and gestures. Then: two teenagers, a boy and a girl, their mouths skewed as they chewed gum; the woman next to them, possibly their mother, biting her lips; and a man standing a distance apart, playing the loner and alternately scratching his belly, then his head. Like all the participants, he had that hopeful, vacant expression of someone certain he was about to be gratified. It made me felt slightly queasy but I stayed near them; I was one of them. I rocked my body gently back and forth, surrendering completely to the sight of the bodies on show: separate bodies, existential bodies, fearful bodies, torn into parts, I saw their eyes and mouths—no longer the real people now, only the painted ones. I saw painted people whose eyes were just sockets, whose eyes did not actually exist. With my own eyes closed, I saw all the upper and lower extremities of the human body in my mind, orifices that existed only to lure us back to our primal physical impulses and which, when they overpowered us, forced us to behave like animals. Then I imagined this behaviour, my eyes shut tight, and abandoned myself to the nightmare, the nightmare of a life in which, at certain extreme moments, our animalistic urges take over: we fall into their clutches, making us act out of pure instinct, an instinct void of morals, an urge capable of boundless beauty, capable of good and evil, of overriding all human limits but, at the same time, being the limit itself. I didn't let the art historian disturb me. She had only just finished talking to an inquisitive, lanky guy before she hurried on, drew herself up in front of a painting and began talking in a shrill, self-important voice. Instead, I hugged myself and rocked my body, imitating what Ines had done when she was sitting in my kitchen. I was overwhelmed by a sharp, brutal insight—that this kind of realization can erupt at any time, in the middle of our everyday lives, in the middle of its gentle flow of connections, on one of those days when, despite the existence of infinity, we arrange flowers in a vase, listen to Mozart or comb our hair.

I was overpowered by a craving for food in a way I hadn't thought possible. I hurried to the exit, almost tripped down the stairs, grabbed my things from the locker and raced, Ines' parka slung over my arm, straight across the small, paved courtyard of the museum and through the revolving doors into the cafe. A cheese roll, I demanded at the counter, and when the young woman picked up the silver tongs to fetch an elaborately prepared roll from the glass display, I quickly pointed to another as well, one with a huge schnitzel inside. The slab of meat was so big that it hung over the sides. That one too, I said, both to take away. She stuck up her nose and made a big deal about looking for a roll of tin foil. It wasn't that kind of cafe, but I had such a strong urge to hold that scrunchy packet in my hands, an urge that no one could spoil—those bread rolls, I knew with a sudden flash of clarity, those bread rolls were mine. Before I'd even reached the exit, I unpacked the one with cheese that had looked so appetizing in the glass cabinet; now it was flattened into a squishy lump but I had never tasted anything so good. I took a large bite without slowing down, walking in the direction of the Main where I thought I'd look for a seat overlooking the river. But that was too far now and I chose the first bench that I came across in an abandoned schoolyard, hiding in the furthermost corner like a predator that wanted its kill all to itself. The tree was kind enough to conceal me in case anyone happened to walk through the iron gates. I finished the first roll in small, quick bites after which I wasn't hungry any more. Perplexed, I weighed the second, bigger tin-foil thing in my hand. What should I do with it? I stuffed it back into my bag in embarrassment, trying to experience the full feeling in my stomach as pleasant, but I couldn't and wished I could bring the food back up. Experimentally, I coughed and gagged a little—but no, the bread roll was clumped in my belly like a solid fist. I decided to walk home as punishment for my gluttony, but I'd forgotten how ugly the footpaths were in Frankfurt, this . . . this . . . —I cast about for a swear word—this un-Rome, un-Paris, un-New York. Then I stood in the middle of the Eiserner Steg footbridge, an icy wind whistling around me and the waves slapping hard against the struts; I stood in the middle of this city that was foreign to me, in my warm but tooshort parka, my legs freezing because I was only wearing thin nylon tights. And I looked out at the River Main, a gurgling mass of black water, a force that flowed out then back on itself, and I suddenly felt as though I too was part of an uncanny river surging forward, as if I would end up in an eddy that I could no longer control. I held on tightly to the railing. I am nothing, I thought. The water must have been full of invisible creatures with eyes that hypnotized me and wanted to pull me under, but they couldn't catch me. I held on tightly to the railing.

I sometimes saw those eyes, and on those occasions, it was better to seek out company. But I didn't know anyone in Frankfurt yet, and so that evening I tried to split myself in two while I walked slowly on. One half was looking after me; the other desperately needed comforting. I stuck my hands into the pockets of Ines' parka and pulled out the business card that Carol had given me. I stared at it for a long time, memorized the address of the advertising agency, then let it flutter down over the edge of the bridge.

The receptionist sat there, as pale and elegant as a wax flower, reading a slim book. Do you have an appointment? she wanted to know, tearing her eyes away from the page with extreme reluctance. The photographers only come here occasionally. No, I said, disappointed. Not only had I come all the way to this ghastly purple villa in Nordend for nothing, I'd also pinned up my hair, painted my lips and worn high heels—the full works. Perhaps the sight made her pity me, all made up to the nines with no appointment; at any rate, she gave me a long, mournful look and pulled the diary towards her while a crease of concentration appeared between her thinly plucked eyebrows. He might be in today, she murmured, Yes, here. Before I could find out when, we were interrupted by a young man with green-tinted sunglasses pushed up on his forehead, who planted himself in front of me. He seemed familiar but I couldn't place him. The shoot on Sunday, he said helpfully, and reached out his hand. I vaguely remembered the scene with the mountain bike—of course, he was the boy in a hurry. Now his tall, lanky figure was dressed in a light-blue suit with a red tie. Paul Flett, he said and when he saw my baffled look—the name of the advertising agency was Flett & Partner—he explained, I'm Flett Junior. Kai hasn't arrived yet but he should be here in half an hour. You might as well come with me and wait. Bye, Doris. Doris nodded and glanced happily back at her green book. I looked at the boy in surprise. What with his suit, his little goatee and the red patches on his neck, he looked scarcely older than a choirboy, but he had everything firmly under control. We went into his office where he sprawled out behind an enormous desk piled with papers. Behind him were some large exotic pot plants which looked as though they were growing out of his shoulders once he sat down. On the light-blue walls hung posters of laughing, stockinged women, flamboyant cars and scent bottles. A mustard-coloured phone sat in front of him. In this environment, Flett Junior looked like a perfect, colourful, venomous fish in its very special habitat. He couldn't sit still for long; first, he shuffled his papers, then turned on an espresso machine that was half-hidden in the plants. I used this brief distraction to flip around a small, framed photo on his desk, expecting to sneak a peek at Flett Junior's smiling girlfriend, but I was wrong. A black-and-white photo showed the villa in a past era. The trees were much smaller, and there were old cars parked on the street; the building wasn't yet painted its conspicuous colour. Flett, who appeared to have eyes in the back of his head, said, my father had it painted purple. That way he could always say: You can't miss it— it's the only purple house in the neighbourhood. That sounds extremely convenient, I said, and thought that the two of them must be very similar. He nudged an espresso cup in my direction. Your father founded the agency? I asked, and we began to make polite conversation. Espresso does you good, he said, and so I obediently drank a second. It was getting easier by the minute to picture him as the boss.

He pointed to some documents on the desk held together with paper clips. A survey on romanticism and consumerism, he said. Astonishing results. Fifty people were interviewed, a cross section of types from a medical assistant to a maths professor, and they all gave completely different answers to the question: What would they do if they wanted to have a romantic moment with their partner? Well, all the answers involved spending money. Isn't that strange? He gave me a long, deep look, as if this was a personal affront. Everyone believes, he carried on, that love is one of the few things in life that has nothing to do with money, but that's not the case at all. No. Flett shook his head. Because how had people replied to the question? They said they went to restaurants, ate meals at home, drank champagne by the fire, took walks in the park, went canoeing, travelled abroad or went for walks on the beach. So? I asked. So, he said, all these things are directly or indirectly linked to consumerism. If you divide them up, they fall into very few categories. There's gastronomy, in other words, buying food to cook at home or going to a restaurant; culture, as in going to the cinema, opera or sports events; or tourism, such as going on holiday.

He sounded more and more resigned, and, as he was speaking, I pictured myself in situations that I thought of as romantic. Sleeping together, I said triumphantly. Sleeping together doesn't fit into any of those categories. Honestly, I thought I was an absolute genius at that moment. But he immediately pointed out my error. And beforehand? he asked in a sad tone of voice. Don't you like a nice glass of champagne? Or to put on sexy lingerie? Hmm, I said. For a while, we sat next to each other, stunned into silence.

After a third espresso, Flett reached for a file, weighed it in his hands with an enigmatic expression and, taking advantage of the momentum of our conversation, asked me: Are you ready for a quick test? I readily agreed—I was starting to like him—and he opened the file. On top lay an advertising image, the kind you often saw, showing a perfect couple sitting together on an expensive sofa in a beautiful living room, the lights dimmed to suggest an evening mood; they were smiling and looking at—well, that was a good question. On the coffee table in front of them was a glowing white crescent of light, about the size of a fist. It looked as though something corrosive had dripped on that part of the photo. May I? I drew in closer and touched it with my finger. It was obviously supposed to be like that. What do you think the light might be? asked Flett. What's the first thing that comes to mind? A cheeseboard, I said, off the top of my head. Interesting, he said, something to eat. Do you want to know what a woman a bit older than you saw? A wedding ring. And her sister saw a bottle of cognac and two glasses. Hmm, I said, feeling caught out, I see where you're heading with this. Everyday obsessions, he said in confirmation, emphasizing every syllable, and then he burst out laughing, a demonic laugh that sounded truly insane and truly uncanny but which was fortunately interrupted by his mobile ringing. Just a minute, he said and went out. I watched him leave, mystified.

I had stood up and started pacing about the room when Kai appeared in the door, camera bags and gear slung around every part of his body. You here? he said, what a surprise. He began to take off his equipment by twisting and turning like an escape artist. I said that Flett Junior had showed me in here and had been very entertaining while I'd been waiting.

And then I got straight to the point: I didn't want Ines to move in with me but I was prepared to meet her now and again. If you think it would do her good, I added. He lowered his head and moved one of the cameras around on the desk while muttering a few clichéd words of thanks. He sounded disappointed but I felt he had no right to be—perhaps he was just tired. The mustard-coloured phone started ringing and before it stopped, I left the room. I would have liked to say goodbye to Flett Junior but he had disappeared. The whole villa was spookily empty and I was happy to hear Doris' voice on the phone, as clear as a bell, in the lobby at the end of the corridor. Her book was lying closed in front of her with a large bookmark sticking out. I looked at the title: *The Dream in the Next Body: Poems*. It was by an author I'd never heard of whose name looked Arabic. Before I closed the door behind me, I caught her saying: Would you like an appointment? She pronounced the word 'appointment' as though it were second nature or a physical reflex, like clearing her throat.

Back home, I paced about my flat on clattering high heels. The telephone rang; I heard Susan's voice and picked up. Hello, I said. Hello? There was silence at the other end but the person didn't hang up. I heard breathing. I listened and heard the click of a lighter, followed by a deep inhalation. There was a long, relaxed silence between us, until one of us—it was hard to tell whom—cut off the connection. We must have hung up at around the same time; I thought I heard the line click at exactly the same moment as I tapped on the little black key with my finger. After the conversation, if it could be described as one, I carried on pacing about the flat. Kitchen, corridor, study, living room. Clatter, clatter, clatter. I was more relaxed now. I stared out of the window and only saw the outline of my face in the glass, a white patch of light. I sat down at my desk. The white patch slid down the glass.

I called Ines. She sounded nervous on the phone, stressing several times that she was happy I had called; I also tried hard to create that impression but the strain on us both left no room to be really happy. We hastily said goodbye.

I went over Ines' words in my head like a water-diviner carefully registering the twitching of her rod. A bar, what had she said again? What was it called? Forgotten. No word on whether Kai would come too. Why would he anyway? Did I have anything to wear? I opened my cupboard and saw heaps of things. I felt sick and excited at the same time, just like I always did when I fell in love with the wrong men. In Rome, I had even been married to one for two years. But enough of the personal details.

In the department store, I took the escalator to the top floor where the designer section was located. Everything there was arranged for maximum elegance: the spacious floor plan, the seating arrangements, the houseplant decor. But the same, imposing showroom dummies stood here as they did elsewhere in the store, with their nasty, long plastic faces.

It was almost empty; apart from me, there were two other women and a little girl crawling on the floor between them. I couldn't work out who the mother was. The women were clearly friends but neither was looking after the child; they were too busy taking turns to show each other all kinds of different clothes. Three sales girls dressed in dark blue took no notice of the women, the child or me, chatting animatedly with one another. I hung a pea-green top and a dark-green skirt over my arm, although the dummy suggested that pea-green was best combined with yellow. Lost in thought, I walked on, picking out the odd item of clothing that took my fancy, taking it off the rail on the hanger and holding it up to take a closer look. As I walked around, I could hear quiet, happy squeaks coming from below. The little girl was hidden under some long evening gowns; in her lap lay a glittery top that she must have pulled down from its hanger to rip off the sequins. She'd already gathered a little pile of them in front of her. Puffing out her cheeks so that she looked like a cherub, she laughed at me. I nodded encouragingly.

The green skirt fitted. I wondered whether it was too short, as it was very short indeed, but also very stylish. I decided to buy it, took it off again and pulled back the changing-room curtain. The little girl had just blown her cover; she was walking on unsteady legs with a fistful of sequins towards the two women who were looking around in shock. Although their panic was silent, it radiated across the room. The trio of shop assistants, who until now had been idle in the corner, rushed over in a perfect line like the Three Fates. One of the shoppers began scolding the girl while the other bent down to pick up the sequins, revealing the areas of responsibility and making it clear who the mother was. I was surprised by the calm, almost approving expression of the mother's friend as she picked up the sequins, as if she would have liked to ruin the top herself. She picked up the little girl, held her close and whispered something into her ear. The mother went away with the sales girls and I saw her write something down. Then the plucked sequin top was put in a plastic bag. The little girl, still in the arms of the friend, had stopped crying by now and was basking in all the attention.

When I left the shop, the street was thronging with people and the sky wasn't as speckled with clouds as earlier on. Further on, in the direction of Römerberg Square, the bakeries and restaurants stood row upon

row. The first lunch-goers were already queuing at
the snack stands. I walked more slowly; I'd eat later,
not now, I could still hold out. Suddenly I heard a
scream that grew louder and more piercing. A man
dressed in chef's whites came running out of the
kitchen door to an Italian restaurant, his hand
pressed to his body, a patch on his tunic colouring
red with blood. Running after him came two other
chefs or kitchen helpers who were trying to calm him
down or look at the wound, but he wouldn't let
them. He rubbed his back against the wall, up and
down, and squealed like an animal. He must have
seriously injured himself or got his hand caught in a
kitchen machine. I felt sick at the idea. Before he
was completely hidden by a crowd of people, I saw
that his tunic was soaked in blood. His screams
stopped—he had surely fainted. Shortly afterwards,
I heard the ambulance sirens and saw the vehicle
driving up through the dense crowd of pedestrians
on Römerberg. I was relieved. At home, I took out
my new things and, wearing them, I lay down on the
sofa to read.

The bar Ines took me to was called Orion Bar, of all
things, but the name didn't fit because the owners
were really stingy with the lighting. It was only eight
in the evening but it may as well have been midnight—
time didn't exist here. The few guests who'd already
arrived were huddled like large dark shadows at
the bar. There's a little dance floor at the back, said

Ines, sitting down, then ordering whisky which the barman put in front of us with polite detachment. Chin-chin, she said. This strange enthusiasm of hers surprised me but I didn't mind; I'd come straight from the newsroom and was tired—I needed a drink. Ines swallowed down her whisky in two satisfied gulps and said, Oh great, they're playing Björk, I have to dance. I watched her take up a spot at the centre of the empty dance floor. Instinctively, she placed herself where the imaginary lines of the room crossed, as if the scene around her had been painted from a central perspective. I found it incredible that she didn't mind dancing on a deserted dance floor where everyone could stare at her—but that's just the way she was, my big sister, always happy to be the centre of attention. She moved slowly to the music. Björk is hard to dance to but she was good at it, moving inside an invisible bell jar. Two other women, encouraged by Ines, stood up as well but neither dared to step into the circle around her: they stayed at the edge. Ines' face was bland and expressionless. Between songs, she stopped dead and didn't move a limb as if she were a robot whose plug had been pulled out, or a showroom dummy, and I thought to myself, She's not dancing for the people watching; she's not dancing for anyone she's thinking about— in fact, she's not even thinking at all. Inside, she's completely empty, moving only for herself in an abstract space created by her dance steps and breathing. That's what made her so beautiful to watch. I'd danced with such abandon just once, not more, and it happened to be the one time I'd taken drugs. It had been late one night when I was a student in a crowded disco in the Trastesvere. I'd gone out with a group from all kinds of faculties including a few medical students; one of them—Enrico or Pedro or Fabio—had given me some pills. Reassured by the fact that he was studying medicine, I swallowed them and soon my perceptions started to change. First, the din of the music and the lopsided, unrhythmical movements of the dancers stopped bothering me; quite the opposite in fact—I suddenly liked them. I even bobbed my head in time to the beat. I remembered picking up my glass from the bar and walking around with it. Then I felt a sudden draught blowing and, without knowing why, I looked around and smiled in all directions. Smiling hurt, as if the nerves it required had been severed where they intersected my brain which was now a deadly quiet capsule. After a while, my surroundings began to transform: first almost imperceptibly around the edges, then picking up speed. A few lights swooped across the dance floor, growing bigger and more intense until they were painful, almost blinding, to look at. Their colours shifted to form a greenish hue, but soon there were no more edges and everything got brighter . . . brighter . . . brighter. I was swept along by the light, and found myself compelled to join the dancers and move in time to the rhythm of the crowd, losing myself in motion. As soon as I hit the dance floor, everything began to glow and seemed eternal, and a feeling welled up in me that was like faith in God or something. Gold—of this I was certain—gold symbolized the flesh of the gods, and mortals writhed on the floor at their feet, thrashing like worms trying to beg favours with their movements. I couldn't keep my feet still because the floor was covered with those small beetles whose name escaped me . . . the name, the name . . . I heard a voice murmuring in my ear, then someone else answered: Scarab. The beetles were rolling dung balls into perfectly round spheres, out of which came eggs, as if from nowhere. My mother was really quick at plaiting my hair, said a lonely-looking woman, pushing past me. Can I hold your hand? a man pleaded, once she'd disappeared. But I knew all he wanted to do was to stick his fingers in my eyes and I dodged away from him, dancing. From outside, the wind was knocking, trying to come in with lightning in tow, spreading an overpowering fragrance of fresh fields of wheat. Everyone was chanting: Hark, the herald angels sing! On all sides, a cheeping could be heard that was issuing from the beetles' mouths, like the cries of tiny children, and I realized that spit was running down everyone's chin, including mine; my chest was heaving and I was no longer sure whether I was awoken from this trance by the sound of my own laughter or because a stranger was shaking me, calling, hey there, hello, can you hear me?

Going down memory lane, eh? the redhead suddenly asked. She had sat down next to me a couple of minutes earlier and was as silent as a mountain at first, her long mane flowing down her back. I know you, she said, brushing a strand of hair off her face, I know you from the shoot. I looked at her for a moment in silence, not sure what she was talking about or why she was breaking the rules of this place, then I asked: What shoot? The Eyewitnesses to History campaign, I showed you into the studio, she replied. So? I asked sceptically, not seeing any reason to renew our acquaintance, but my rebuff didn't bother her in the slightest. It's funny, that's all, she said good-humouredly and swirled her glass so that the ice cubes clinked. She was getting on my nerves and I thought about just getting up and going over to the dance floor but quickly dropped the idea. I would simply ignore her instead. I stared into my drink as if contemplating whether I should jump in. My name is Carol, by the way, in case you've forgotten. Ah, that's Ines dancing over there, isn't she adorable? She shifted closer to me, so close that I could smell her perfume, an awful, flowery scent that I might have found amusing had I been in a better mood. Carol, I don't know what you're on about. Ines has a boyfriend—and I'm not into women either, so just knock it off. Knock what off? She gazed at

me with her penetrating dark eyes. And anyway, even
if Ines has a boyfriend, I did get together with her,
just for a while, but long enough for that sister of
yours to break my heart . . . And as if to prove the
passion of her feelings, a little ember of ash fell from
her cigarette onto the Formica counter, burning a
small hole. It's almost a year ago now but I'm still
not over it. What hurts most is that she says she can't
remember a thing. Perhaps because nothing happened in the first place, and, besides, even if it did,
what do you want from her anyway? I replied. Carol
sighed and said, Nothing, nothing at all, just to
watch her dance, she's here and she's such a good
dancer, and then I often bring her home. I found this
last remark very odd, so odd in fact that I conde-
scended to ask: You do *what*? Carol gave me a disdainful look. I can see that you don't know much
about what's going on around here. There are things
that Ines just can't remember. I couldn't help laughing
suddenly because this conversation was so absurd,
but then I looked over at the dance floor and saw
that Ines had disappeared; only the two girls were
left, dancing at the edge. The centre of the dance floor
was empty, conspicuously so, because no one dared
enter the circle of light, as if it still belonged to Ines.
I looked around frantically, with no clue where she
could have gone. Suddenly I was angry with Carol—
it was her fault. In a bristling tone, I asked whether
she'd seen Ines leave. Carol scanned the room with

an air of self-importance and said: No, she hasn't left, she's over there, having a drink with some guy, I have a good instinct when it comes to her, I can always find her. This thought gave her the smug look of some expert who has just proven she is the best in her field, head and shoulders above the rest. What do you mean, some guy? Has Kai turned up? I asked, craning my neck. Ines was standing next to a man who looked as if he liked to party hard and might have been twenty or, just as easily, forty. When she saw me, she waved and came over with a glass of whisky filled to the brim. He bought me a drink, she mumbled indistinctly, and then seemed to spot Carol. What a surprise, Carol, she said. I looked at Ines. The way she'd pronounced Carol sounded more like *Crol*. She obviously noticed this and tried to get a grip on herself. Ca-rol, this is my sister. She's had a hard day at the office and we're partying a little and, yes, I'm a little bit drunk . . . She lost her train of thought, but the next sip helped. Just a bit, she said, looking over at the dance floor and pulling a troubled face. Those people dancing are terribly young . . . She blew a high-proof cloud of breath into my face; I turned away involuntarily and, although it was pointless, corrected her, saying that I hadn't had a particularly hard day at the office, just the average kind. Ah-ha, said Carol, looking at me amusedly. Perhaps we should go home, I suggested. Ines said, Exactly, home, and clambered with difficulty onto the bar stool where she swayed into a sitting position and then took a pretty little hip flask out of her handbag. After confessing, she had lost all her inhibitions. I saw her mobile flashing in her bag and asked, Listen, didn't you say that Kai was coming? He could pick us up, right? Call him, OK? Oh, yeah! replied Ines and pressed two buttons. Hello? she shouted, then added more sheepishly, Yes, exactly, you know, no, the Orion Bar. After that, she didn't say anything for a long time. Then she turned to me, mumbling, He wants to speak to you, and held out the phone. Me? I asked, taken aback, and took the phone with trembling hands. I couldn't help noticing how interested Carol was in all this. Is that you? he asked, in a grave, guarded tone, but his voice was so familiar that it startled me and everyone could hear the uncertainty in my voice when I answered, Yes, hello, I'm here with Ines. I left Carol out; she thought she was so important anyway, standing there with her flashing eyes and tugging her fingers all the time through her red mane. What a thrill she must get from all this—at least as exciting as being at the cinema. I backed off a few steps with Ines' mobile, burying the little device under my hair, and pulled my head in tight—all this to persuade myself that I was having a private phone call. I lowered my voice, just like I would have done had I been alone, and asked: Kai, can you hear me? The evening's already over, unfortunately. I tried to sound amused. I noticed how tired

I was all of a sudden, fit to drop. Is she very drunk? Kai wanted to know. I mean, can she still walk? You know, I'm not really into playing the chauffeur for the umpteenth time. A colleague of mine is at my place, sitting in the other room, and I still have to develop some films for tomorrow. So I have a lot to do . . . can't you drive? I explained that I didn't know where Ines had parked and that I probably couldn't find my way home, but that we could take a taxi. And then the conversation seemed to be over, which was fine by me as I had a sudden urge to yawn—I had a real yawning fit, in fact. But now Kai had started talking, he just wouldn't stop. He was sorry, he said, he felt guilty that my evening had been ruined; Ines shouldn't call him until the morning. My God, he said, I'm sick to death of her slurred phone calls, I hate it all so much! During my yawning solo, he improvised an aggressive monologue. I see, I said warily, my mouth still half open, and he carried on: OK, listen, I'll finish up here and then come by her place, can you please stay with her until I get there? I'll see my colleague off and, oh yes, give her lots of water to drink. My God, I sound like a professional social worker, and in case you were going to ask, no, it's not the first time this has happened. When our conversation finally ended, I said exhaustedly, We're taking a taxi. Ines asked tearfully, Why won't he come? I fished out a fifty and a twenty-euro note from my purse and realized I was going to have to say goodbye to both of them: Ines had had a lot to drink and this wasn't a cheap bar. Having said that, I've run out of money, I said, embarrassed. We'll have to stop at a cash machine on the way. That was Carol's cue. She heaved her Rubenesque figure off the bar stool and announced, I'll give you a lift, looking at Ines as if she wanted to devour her with her eyes. So odd in a way, I thought, because the way Ines stood there, she was just a shadow of her former self, and then I realized I was jealous. Incredible, I thought, people are such idiots, and I was no exception.

Ines insisted on finishing her drink before she was ready to go, which in her case meant zigzagging through the room, straight down the middle and back across the dance floor. Could you make it any more obvious? I murmured. I saw her drinking companion grinning at us. This made me sad and angry at the same time, as he seemed to know Ines well, or at least the problem. Carol, who had got her second wind, said, Oh, come on, it doesn't matter. As long as she doesn't throw up all over my car. Can you sit in the back with her and tell me if she starts doing anything weird? I hissed something back in agreement. Really, she almost sounded as if she was enjoying all this; or perhaps I was being unfair to her and she was just excited to be so close to Ines again. The icy air outside slapped me in the face. I felt my frosty nose, my lips and the cold creeping up my body. Carol had a sports car the colour of ox blood with reddish-brown leather seats; it looked brand new. Ines, who I'd manoeuvred into the narrow back seat with difficulty, was giving off a sour odour from the alcohol, and, as soon as we'd sat down, she rested her head against my shoulder. Mingled with the smell of the leather seats and the heating, which Carol now switched on, I felt as if I were in the belly of some large animal, a monster that would first digest my sister, then me. Carol looked in the rear-view mirror at my disgusted expression and remarked, You're not really used to this, are you? Bringing her home and all that? With an effort I said, No, we haven't seen each other for   a few years, I didn't know that she had, well, gone this way. Carol laughed, said: That's a nice way of putting it, and kept her eye on me in the mirror. Well, she said, when we had to stop for a red light at a brightly lit crossing, I never thought I'd get mixed up with an alcoholic. It's a bad idea—they're like moths, always crashing into the same window, they never learn. But that's love for you. The interior of the car was steeped in the amber glow from the traffic light; there were no other cars to be seen. Meanwhile, Ines' head had ended up on my lap. Her skin shimmered pinkly, her hair red: she looked perfectly otherworldly. Carol would have surely liked the way she looked and in fact kept desperately searching for a glimpse of my sister's face in the mirror as she drove, but eventually gave up when she caught sight of me mimicking her love-struck expression. I have the feeling you're mistaken about what love is, I said. Love is reciprocal. What you're talking about is infatuation at best and, at worst, obsession. I observed her robust back, clad in a padded denim jacket, saw her shrug, then lean almost imperceptibly to the side as she took a sharp left like a rally driver.

We arrived not long afterwards, and Carol wanted to accompany us but I said no, thanked her politely for the lift home and then, with great difficulty and effort, clambered out of the car, pushing Ines in front of me. Carol wasn't angry; she may have lost this battle but she could still win the war, and there was a great deal left for her to do: this was her mission, her obsession. Alexander the Great had cried when there were no worlds left for him to conquer; Carol didn't think this was necessary. See you soon, she said, nodding and beaming. Her car was barely out of sight when I thought, dammit, I could really use someone's help. Ines' ankles buckled and she sat down on the kerb. I opened my arms and pulled at her, this bundle reeking of alcohol, to stop her landing spreadeagled on the ground. Sorry, said Ines dolefully, and I said in a soothing tone, You don't have to be, come on, let's wave Carol goodbye. I talked to her as if she were a small child, and Ines really did wave down the empty street while tears welled up in her eyes. Good old Carol, she mumbled, good old

Carol, I do love her. Then she didn't want to say anything else, least of all where she'd stowed her front-
door key, and, when she didn't reply, I started to
rummage around in her handbag, then searched the
pockets of her leather jacket, hoping that no one
would walk down the street at that moment and see
me groping about her in this strange way.

I steered Ines into her flat which was smaller than
mine and furnished in a completely loveless way. I
was surprised how the furniture stood about like a
group of awkward acquaintances, a lone chair in the
middle of the room. The sofa had been pulled out a
few feet from the wall as if someone had lost something behind it and not pushed it back again. Ines
flopped down on it straight away. She murmured
something that sounded like, I feel sick. Water, I
thought, remembering what Kai had said, and went
into the kitchen. There I found a whole line-up of
empty bottles—rum, whisky, all sorts. I opened the
fridge and stared at a single illuminated lemon. That
can't be all there is, I thought and looked into the
freezer compartment; and true enough, a bottle of
vodka nearly rolled into my arms.

When I came back with a glass of water, Ines had
stood up and was walking unsteadily towards me. I
rushed over to her like a nurse. Ines, I said, Ines. I
wanted to ask her how often this kind of thing happened, but there was no point, not now, so all I said

was, Here, drink this, and she took a sip like a good girl. More, yes, drink it, it'll stop you feeling sick. I forced a second glass down her and she sank back down on the sofa. Is that better, Ines? But she'd already fallen asleep and was snoring softly like a little cartoon mouse. A strange sense of relief, almost satisfaction, overcame me as I, feeling shattered, sat down on the armchair next to her. For a moment, it seemed as if I'd planned this chore of putting Ines to bed, as if it had been marked in my diary for some time. I stood up and fetched myself a glass of water too. This time I didn't turn on the kitchen light. It was slowly dawning on me that there really were building works going on here, not in front of Ines' flat but in the middle of it. Her life was messier and more torn up than any street under repair. I went to sit beside her and listened to her breathing. Red blotches marred her face as if she were allergic to some ingredient in the drink, or perhaps to her very existence. She looked more fragile and vulnerable than ever, and I sat down next to her, trying to put my emotions in order. A moment before, I'd felt important, like a worthy saviour, but this impression had vanished and now I felt nothing but emptiness. Although I was awake and sober and didn't have red blotches on my face, it was as if I were looking into a mirror. So that was your secret, I whispered; that's what you wanted to tell me and not tell me at the same time, damn it.

I must have dozed off; in any case, I flinched when the doorbell rang, and Ines was startled too. Her gaze darted all over the room for a few seconds, found me, and confusion flitted across her face. Like an annoyed nanny, I found myself thinking, Who dares disturb her in her sleep? Then I remembered Kai, and went over to the door, quickly raking my fingers through my hair and smoothing down my skirt. Kai was standing there in a black, unbuttoned coat and tousled hair, like an avenging angel. Where is she? Before I could answer, he tore past me and found her. He barely looked at her, just said, It's better if we put her to bed and undress her; and because he said we, I realized I was supposed to help. So I followed him as he carried her into the bedroom, where he immediately took on a commanding tone: Please fetch a couple of towels from the bathroom, let's cover the pillows just in case. I obeyed. No, this definitely wasn't the first time he'd done this: his movements showed a practised hand. He sat her up and yanked the pullover over her head, then rolled down her tights, all very quickly and efficiently. I assisted, propping up her torso, amazed at how heavy she was all of a sudden. Earlier in the car, she'd seemed so light, but now, tangled up in her underwear, she no longer seemed otherworldly but earthly instead, like a sleek, heavy animal. I gave Kai a sidelong look, thinking he must find her helplessness very arousing. But no, he just seemed frustrated. He roughly pulled off her things as if she were a doll that couldn't feel anything. Soon she was dressed in nothing but her knickers and bra, and I wondered if he would stop, but he didn't. I looked away in embarrassment when her nipples were exposed and, without wanting to, I compared the shape of her breasts with mine, her legs with my legs. And then we were finished, like a couple of parents who had finally got their difficult baby off to sleep. We stood at the foot of Ines' bed and looked down at her. I noticed the strange expression that she had taken on all at once. When had that happened? It must have been while we were undressing her. I really couldn't interpret her strange look. I examined her face as if she were an insect under a magnifying glass. What on earth was it? And then I realized that she looked satisfied, as if she were happy with herself and her defeat, and I felt as if I recognized her again, the way she used to be: unpredictable and capricious, moody, exhausting and inimitable. Everyone loved her. Kai turned and I wanted to tear myself away too but then she opened her eyes. Thank you for everything, she whispered, barely audible. Kai said nothing but I whispered, It's all right, you get some rest, and that seemed to satisfy her because she obediently closed her eyes.

You don't have to be so nice to her, Kai snapped when we were back in the living room, and I stared at him; the situation had been turned on its head. He sat down on the sofa where the hollow made by Ines' head was still visible, but he'd hardly taken a seat when he jumped back up again. Sorry, now I'm taking out my anger on you when I should be thanking you. I was confused, no, you shouldn't, I said, it goes without saying. I tried to make it sound natural, as if I put at least ten drunken sisters to bed every evening after getting home from a bar; at the same time, on a subconscious level, I was starting to grasp the magnitude of the catastrophe, more through Kai and Carol's behaviour than through Ines'. Kai sat down next to me. His closeness confused me, our sudden complicity made me feel unsure. Embarrassed, I folded my hands, then stood up to put them in my trouser pockets—once, twice—until I realized that I was wearing my new skirt that had no pockets. She's sick, he said, and then, as if continuing this train of thought: I'd like a drink but I guess there's nothing left. There's some vodka in the freezer compartment, I said, quite the housewife, I can fetch it. And because he didn't react, neither agreeing nor disagreeing, I went into the kitchen and grabbed the bottle, which froze my palms and left fingerprints on the foggy glass. I poured a generous measure, at least for him. But the drink didn't calm him down at all. He prowled around the room. You know, I can't go on like this much longer. I used to believe her excuses about why she was hammered after one or two glasses of wine—like, she hadn't eaten all day, or had been at the gym for two hours and that's why the alcohol had gone to her head. At some point, though, I realized that she'd already had a few by the time she came over to my place, supposedly for dinner. But food doesn't interest her. She hardly eats a thing and we end up drinking instead. He paused for a moment, picturing it all. And then there's the split second when she changes into someone else. Her brain goes berserk and she's controlled by one ugly emotion—I can never tell what it's going to be: anger, aggression or self-pity . . . because there's never any connection to what's just happened. It's completely random. She's taken over by an alien force—I call it the hour between dog and wolf. She might end up smashing the furniture or going after me with a knife. In that instant she hates herself so much that she attacks anyone near her, and you can count yourself lucky that it didn't happen tonight—she was tame. True, she wasn't aggressive, I agreed quietly, clasping my cold glass. She was sweet the whole time, even when she wasn't there all of a sudden, but that only lasted for ten to fifteen minutes at most. She didn't do anything. Once I'd started, I felt like I had to talk, talk non-stop, keep talking and explain the reason for this . . . this feeling of being a nobody; this must be the feeling that caused Ines to drink, a feeling that our father had handed down to us—I'd thought just to me, but now a few things were becoming clear. However, I was unable to speak. And even if I'd been able to, how could I have put it? Yes, Kai said, not there, then she's completely out of it, and I nodded even though I hadn't meant it like that, not in the figurative sense. He began to pace up and down again like an injured animal that suspects its pain is somewhere in the room. It drove me crazy but I didn't say anything, trying instead to concentrate on his face as a way to stop him, an elegant but wild face, which you might think was just the way he wanted to look, just a little less tired perhaps. He carried on talking, his gaze fixed on the floor. Recently, on my birthday, she lost it completely. She'd hardly come in the door when she started hurling one accusation after the next, and it got weirder and weirder, and while she was screaming at me, the bones around her mouth jutted out, like on an X-ray picture that's too bright, and you won't believe it but she threw a glass at me, it missed my face by an inch. I can't tell anyone this, no one believes me, and even if I could, how would it make her look? I hesitated, then eventually said: That's terrible. I hated myself for the way I said it. It was as though I didn't like her any more than usual, as though I didn't have one iota of sympathy for her, and was just faking something for Kai and me. I was no longer sure myself. I began to think out loud. Up until now, she'd always managed to cope with her problems. No matter what had happened, she could turn them into something positive for herself or her art. I despised and admired her for it . . . I thought for a moment. Did I really admire her for it?

I closed my eyes and saw an ugly, yellow colour. *I am nothing.* Kai didn't react to what I'd said. But I can't leave her, he said, I mean, not that I want to, but I can't even threaten her with it. I looked him in the eye and, at that moment, seeing his panic—a mixture of agitation and pain on his face—I wanted to go over and touch him, hug him, not because I wanted to comfort him but because I desired him. He carried on pacing and I couldn't stop wondering what it would be like to sleep with him. If there's anything I can do, I'm willing to help, I said, and Kai said, Yes, if only I knew how. I knew from the beginning that you were sound, he said, taking one, or even two steps towards me, and I imagined straight away that he too felt the tension between us, a tangible sexual energy. But I was wrong. He just said, Sorry, I just have to get my wallet from the hallway, I still owe you money for the taxi. For the taxi? I repeated. Was he being serious? For starters, I yelled after him, my sister can pay for herself, and secondly, Carol drove us home! Yes, incredible, huh? Carol was there, as quick as a flash, when you didn't show up. He appeared in the doorframe. Carol? he said softly. Of course, Carol. Her girlfriend makes fantastic films, she's really talented, incredible films. Horror—if you like horror, that is . . . He mumbled something else, then turned to go. It almost hurt to see him leave. I wanted to touch his back but of course I didn't. I went into Ines' kitchen with my untouched vodka. I rummaged about and found two plastic bags which

I crammed with fifteen empty bottles to take to the recycling container. I was putting off leaving even though I knew I'd be going soon. Eventually, I wrote a note. Dear Ines, please get in touch soon. I couldn't think of anything else. I drew a smiley underneath, then I left the flat, the bottles clinking in the bags. The door banged shut behind me, like the lid of a coffin.

Four days later, I was coming back from the hairdresser. Yet again, it was dark. I crossed Eschenheim Green, then walked, after wavering briefly, through a section of the park. I went past a lit-up snack bar and saw through the window some teenage boys hanging about inside; then I passed a kiosk surrounded by hunched men. Despite the cold, they were standing outside, drinking beer. All at once, one of them broke away and came towards me, getting so close that I could smell the reek of alcohol on his breath. I was about to back off when a familiar voice said my name, and a pale, slightly haughty face squinted into mine. It took me a while to recognize him, the way you recognize an object held too close to your face; it was my colleague, Richard Bartholomäi, who had been off sick for the past three days. He was the one who only dressed in Armani suits that went very well with his generally arrogant manner, and the grubby tracksuit that he now wore was a shocking transformation. A shopping basket on his arm was filled with four bottles of beer and a packet of nuts, and there were stains on the sleeves of his tracksuit jacket. But this didn't stop him from eyeing me in a critical, even disdainful way. While I was still trying to remember whether we'd been on first or second-name terms the few times we'd met at the coffee machine, he took the decision out of my hands, called me by my first name and said how different I looked, an allusion to my new hairstyle. I smiled and shot back, So do you. He told me about his plans for the evening, which amounted to sitting in front of the TV with a stack of beers, watching videos. He explained this to me in a very charming, roundabout way, as if the sheer ordinariness of it was something special. Only when he openly invited me to join him did I get what he was driving at. I was surprised and took a little step in his direction; he took a full leap in mine. But I didn't hesitate—what was there to do at home after all? For a moment he looked surprised, then turned businesslike. I'd better fetch a couple more beers then, he said. He had a laid-back way of walking in his trainers, as if stepping on a cloud rather than tarmac on this cold winter's night. Perhaps I too should take a few days off soon, I thought, get some fresh air. He knocked on the window of the kiosk. Behind it sat the type of kiosk woman of whom it was hard to tell whether she was still alive or simply hadn't yet been found. Her prehistoric head sat flush on her shoulders like a tortoise's. When Richard knocked on the pane, the head moved feebly. She wasn't the least bit happy about being disturbed and looked reluctantly through the window like a terrarium animal that felt we were intruders. I looked at the stains on Richard's sleeve when he reached into the shopping basket for his wallet while as I hopped from one leg to the other. It was incredible how cold I suddenly felt, and the last thing I was in the mood for was drinking beer. I wondered whether I'd prefer Richard to change his clothes as soon as we arrived at his flat as a sign of respect, or stay the way he was, which would be just as respectful, as that way, he'd be showing me I wasn't intruding on his sloppy-joe mood and that he felt comfortable enough to show me: a win-win situation. I followed him: he looked like Little Red Riding Hood with his shopping basket on his arm, carefully jockeying his way into the entrance hall, two buildings to the right of the kiosk. The light's broken, sorry, he said. I flinched when, without warning, his hand touched mine, but he only wanted to show me where the bannister was—he was just being practical, as if tidying something away. This triggered a sudden desire in me, which was idiotic considering his tracksuit and the fact that I'd never really noticed him in the office.

Here we are. He showed me into a bright, warm hallway. On the floor lay a red children's digger and a robot; on the wall hung a photograph of Richard, a woman laughing and a small boy. Should I be quiet?

I whispered, pointing at the toys. Richard looked pensively at the digger and said, No, Leonard's already been picked up by his mother. He's with her this weekend. He bent down and parked the digger under the telephone table. I spoke at normal volume again. Leonard, that's a nice name. Still staring at the digger, lost in thought, or rather at the telephone table that now hid the digger, Richard said, we named him after Leonidas, a brand of Belgian pralines. We met in Brussels in a confectionery shop. We've only just split up. He offered me a clothes hanger. We parted very amicably, he added. I gave him my coat and looked at the photo on the wall. The boy, who was standing next to his smiling mother, had chocolate-brown curls and shiny skin that looked like fresh milk, so he did look quite like a praline. They're very beautiful, both of them, I said, and Richard replied very softly, almost inaudibly, gently tapping his finger on the smiling woman's face, Who needs reason when you have charm. Sorry? I asked, looking at him uncomprehendingly, and he said, Oh, never mind.

Like Richard, the living room was in a state of slight disarray. The coffee table was strewn with newspapers, empty cigarette and trail-mix packets, and dirty glasses with dregs of red wine. The sofas were draped with washing—T-shirts, socks and tea towels. She took the laundry rack with her, explained Richard, as he began folding underpants. I took over the tea towels and T-shirts and we worked silently side by side, feeling awkward at this sudden intimacy. Not much later, when I came back from the kitchen where I'd taken the dirty glasses, the room had been transformed. Without the laundry, I could see what nice, light-coloured leather sofas Richard had. He'd also put on some lamps that showed off how big and friendly the room was. There were some white woollen rugs on the slightly worn parquet floor that I tentatively crossed towards him. Have a seat, said Richard, pointing to the spot beside him; a bottle of beer was already open and waiting for me on the freshly wiped glass-top table. He reached into his basket again, which he'd put beneath the table, and if I bent forward and looked down, I could see his movements, as if I were looking into a very clear pond. I saw him reach for the shiny packet of nuts. He emptied its contents into a blue ceramic bowl and pushed them towards me, leaning back comfortably.

Have you never thought it strange that the big, heavy nuts in these mixtures always end up lying on top? It doesn't make any sense when you first notice, he began, weighing a few nuts in his hand. I shook my head to show he had guessed quite rightly that I had never even given this a thought. The nuts, he explained, leave the factory all mixed up, but en route, all that bumping about in crates and boxes on ships and trucks separates them again. Every jolt loosens the mixture into various sizes and the smaller ones slip between the gaps underneath the big ones, so they end up on top. The result: cashew and peanuts at the bottom, Brazil nuts on top. A German–American team researched this for the food industry and christened it the Brazil Nut Effect. He paused to clear his throat. The Brazil Nut Effect is important, and can be used in the mixing and demixing production of medicine, sorting grains or food production. In the physics of granular material, the Brazil Nut Effect has the same importance as the fruit fly for gene research. A tender expression flitted across his face. The Brazil Nut Effect, I repeated, in a soft voice.

As he was talking, softly and amicably, the blue bowl passed between us several times like a freighter between two countries with progressively improving trade relations; now and again, we took a sip of beer. It took me a while to pick *Frankenstein's Bride* from the films he had. I'd already watched some of them whereas others didn't interest me much. Richard left the room for a moment. When he came back, he was wearing a black T-shirt and black jeans and smelled faintly of aftershave. Even as the opening credits were rolling, we held hands, and, during the first scene, when Frankenstein wanders about the cemetery, we started kissing. It looked like a good film. I glanced at the screen now and then and saw that the monster had to cross a deep, gloomy valley; he was very lonely. During the really sad part with the blind violinist, my body went limp out of pity. But Richard managed to create a kind of tension in me again for which I was grateful. The climax of events, as far as I could make out, was the scene where the terrible bride, created especially for Frankenstein, rejects him to the sound of much rattling and hissing. It's a great scene but the last one I saw, because in our case things were progressing in the opposite direction. I was Richard's bride, at least for that evening, and I turned my back on the film and fully embraced my part. It was a woman's role that would have been alien to me in a different state of mind: she was very much in need of love and ready to respond to every thrust, tug and plea, and clearly show what she wanted in return. The two of us, Richard and I, did our best to become a couple and share some feelings—not love, admittedly, but affection and desire—and we were both pleased with ourselves afterwards. We looked at each other, relaxing after this successful event, the achievement of a task efficiently divided between colleagues to the satisfaction of both parties. We laughed, and he put his arm around me. You're not the least bit ill, I said later after we'd rested for a while in silence. And I fancied I saw the corner of his mouth twitching slightly, although he continued to pretend he was asleep.

At night, I used the bathroom. The shelf over the sink was cluttered with women's cosmetics and make-up. I studied the brand names: Shiseido, Estée Lauder, Jade, Lancôme, Lagerfeld. It was certainly a strange kind of woman who'd left him: one who had taken their son and the laundry rack but had left her make-up. I put some on, then quietly gathered my clothes that were strewn about the living room. I walked into the dark hallway, lighting my way with the feeble glow given off by my mobile when I flipped it open, as I couldn't find the light switch. In farewell, I swept my display across the photos on the wall and the red digger under the telephone table: I wasn't in any hurry. Noiselessly and without stumbling, I found my way to the front door and down the dark corridor. With a smile on my lips, I walked through the city at night, and with every step I became more awake and cheerful.

By the time I arrived home, I was in a very good mood; and although it was the middle of the night, I began sorting my Post-its. The one with the hairstylist's address, clearly a good-luck charm, got pride of place on the coat-stand mirror in the hallway, and then I lay on my bed for a while without turning the light on, staring into the darkness. I hadn't closed the curtains and the room was occasionally lit up by the headlights of a passing car. I watched the lights slide over the wall: they appeared and disappeared, appeared and disappeared. I couldn't tell when the next one was coming although I was sure there would be one, as surely as I knew that cars existed, even if I didn't own one. Damn, cars existed, as well as films that I fell asleep in the middle of, and films that I had

sex in the middle of, and films that I watched on my
own, just for the sheer hell of it, in a good mood, in
a cinema in Rome or Frankfurt. And tomorrow I
would go swimming; swimming pools existed as
well, yes, they did; and before I could get to lakes,
oceans and mountains, still in my clothes, slightly jit-
tery and with faint car headlights passing over me
that now appeared more regularly, as it was already
six in the morning, I fell, in the middle of my list, into
a vast, deep sleep.

The alarm clock went off barely an hour later. I
wasn't quite awake when I staggered into the bathroom, and when I came out again I didn't feel much
better but I didn't mind. I liked my semi-conscious
state that morning, which turned the day into a
continuation of the previous one, everything taking
twice as long as usual. I was on the late shift that day
and didn't have to be in the newsroom until lunchtime, which was wonderful. When the phone rang, I
immediately picked up; Ines' voice greeted me. She
said that Carol had invited us to dinner and, taken
by surprise, I agreed to go. It was already arranged
for the following day, which threw me, but OK.
When the phone rang a second time, I picked up
before Susan's voice came on; but this time it wasn't
Ines, it was Richard, who sounded very calm, as if
he'd slept well, and who asked me warmly if I was
free the following day. I said, sorry I can't make it.
The day after tomorrow? It was arranged. So, having

already made quite a few plans, I set off for work. In an upbeat mood, I said to myself: Good, something different for a change.

When Ines had called to say that Carol was inviting us to dinner, I'd automatically assumed that she'd meant at Carol's place. But in the car, Ines corrected me: No, no way, Carol always says that she only cooks for her enemies. We're going to what's supposed to be the best Thai place in town. She was driving Kai's car. She steered slowly and not very confidently, always concerned that I was fine—with the heating, with the way she took corners—she even said I was allowed to smoke. But I declined and she returned to what lay ahead of us—where the best Thai food in the city was, that kind of thing. These were safe topics and I let her talk, absorbed in my own thoughts. Not a word about the episode in the Orion Bar, not a peep—it had never happened.

The restaurant's decor was self-assuredly ugly. Someone had thought it a good idea for the diners to feast their eyes on rows of Buddhas, masks and monkey gods that hung from the walls and ceiling; the latter, especially, stared down disapprovingly at the guests. But Carol and the woman with her, already waiting at the table, scrutinized Ines and me even more intently. Hello, said Carol, giving Ines a long look. Then she gestured to her companion and struck up an official tone. Ines, it's my pleasure to introduce you to my girlfriend, Rebecca. She's a film academic. Interesting, said Ines, and we sat down. What do you do exactly? I asked Rebecca, remembering what Kai had said about how talented Carol's girlfriend was. She answered politely but with badly concealed reluctance, making it clear that she'd explained this at least a hundred times before: I'm working on the aesthetics of 70s horror films. And I make my own films. As she said this, she raked her fingers through her short hair with a bored gesture. I saw that her fingernails were short and bitten down and, thinking of Richard, I said, Interesting, I know someone you should meet. He has an enormous collection of horror films. At this, she rolled her eyes in annoyance. God, all these self-appointed experts who think that if they stare at the TV all night, that makes them film specialists. I looked at her, slack-jawed at this open snub. She had the voice of the future professor who would make a name for herself—huskily erotic and resolute—but besides her voice, everything about her was ascetic. Her sinewy body was clad in jeans and a polo shirt, the exact opposite of Carol who was flaunting her ample décolleté in a velvet dress which seemed a little over the top for the occasion. Carol laid her hand, covered in silver rings, on Rebecca's bony fingers; but Rebecca pulled them away immediately. Let's order, she said, and flipped open the menu with determination. Carol turned to Ines and said, Well, sweetie, what are you having?

Her behaviour was strangely jovial. I stared in confusion at the blur of numbers and signs—the sheer quantity of dishes on offer felt like a threat right then. When I looked up, I saw Rebecca's grey eyes focussed on me: reptilian eyes, old and rotten to the core. She could see through me to tucked-away places where my deepest fears were hidden. I quickly looked down again but I knew that she wouldn't miss a thing, especially the fact that Ines wasn't drinking. No beer, really? asked Rebecca, And you, Carol? She shook her head, I'll just have a mango lassi like Ines. Rebecca pulled a face. I'll have tea, I said, but when the little Thai waitress came over to take our order, Rebecca ordered four glasses of champagne without consulting us. I shot an anxious look at Ines but she seemed to sense it and deliberately avoided looking my way. She too had worked out that this Rebecca tuned in on every detail; it was obvious in the way she moved her head in agreement or dismissal, already quite the lecturer handing out grades. She wasn't here just for the fun of it. The place was packed to the rafters. I fidgeted in my chair, looking at the groups to the left and right: all families or close friends who seemed relaxed as they nibbled at their food. Our table was the only one where distrust and tough bargaining reigned: four women, all strangulating one another. I seriously began to think up an excuse to leave this get-together on the spot. I'd already left many other unpleasant gatherings, in all kinds of cities, on official and informal occasions, and people had always managed very well in my absence. But the longer I hesitated, the more my chance to leave diminished until, suddenly, it was too late. Because now Carol was making a toast: to us all, she said, to you, Ines, to you—she nodded at me— and to you, Rebecca. She kissed Rebecca on the lips. I had a dream about this, Carol said. We were all sitting here talking like we are now, she said gaily, her red hair glowing. And that's why I invited you. Ines nodded, lost in thought, as if none of this concerned her. Grimly, Rebecca shuffled the soya sauce, toothpicks and condiment pots around in ever-changing formations. I seemed to be the only one who cringed at the thought that we were re-enacting a scene from Carol's dreams. I cleared my throat. You can all help yourself to my vegetables, said Carol and shovelled some onto my plate. I stared at them in annoyance, having considered the edge of my plate to be a natural boundary until now. Carol shrugged, offended, and began to pile broccoli and mushrooms onto Rebecca's plate; Rebecca immediately began to shovel it all down with mechanical movements, a robot tuned to a tediously dull programme at the highest speed. I thrust the vegetables under my rice, then the rice under the chicken, and, when I had finished, I turned it all over again. Do you know what Gwyneth Paltrow's diet consultant says to her? Rebecca's grey eyes were on me. She wasn't smiling; her thin lips were shiny with grease. No idea, I said. She says she should only ever eat naked in front of the mirror;

that way she can see for herself the effect each food
has on her body. Rebecca opened her mouth to laugh
and I saw her pink tongue and healthy teeth. I put
my chopsticks to one side. She wallowed in her victory. Or is it that you just don't like it? she probed.
She could barely contain her glee at my surrender.
No, I don't like it, I replied, at which she shot back,
Well, I think it's very good. I didn't say it wasn't
good, I explained, just that I didn't like it. There's a
difference. My god, she's a puritan, Rebecca said to
no one in particular, don't you find that boring?
Carol couldn't help herself—she was staring at Ines.
I caught Rebecca's furious look. It was too soon for
her to overlook that this woman had shared Carol's
bed and turned up in her dreams. In fact, while Carol
tried to make peace with everyone in her clumsy
manner, Rebecca's hatred for her rival was only
beginning to warm up. I asked Rebecca whether it
was creepy to do a doctorate in horror films, and if
she had nightmares. I asked her in a silly, childish
voice just to annoy her, curious to see how she'd
ward me off. She replied that the interesting thing
about horror films was their straightforward way of
dealing with the problems of the era they were set
in—and that they still made her feel something in this
world in which everyone had become completely
numb. People take all kinds of drugs these days, she
said, looking at Ines, who, surprised by this attack,
set down the forkful of food that she'd just lifted to

her mouth and reached for her champagne for the first time. Well, she said, and took a sip. I couldn't do it, I said to Rebecca, stepping up as her sparring partner again, I couldn't watch those kinds of things. I'd be afraid that all that ugliness would seep into me. Rebecca pretended to consider this. Well, I'm not sure whether ugliness and beauty are that far apart . . . but you see where the problem lies: everyone thinks they have something to say when it comes to a popular medium like film, and then the discussion gets watered down. She took a last mouthful and, with a snort, pushed her empty plate away.

I excused myself for a moment, but didn't go to the bathroom; instead, I walked outside onto the deserted, rain-slick pavement. It did me good to be out there for a moment without my coat, waiting until my hands turned cold and my sanity told me to go back in, no matter what was waiting for me there. But I stayed, thrust my hands into my trouser pockets and stared at the light reflected in the puddles while image after image flashed through my mind, none of which I managed to hold on to. A second bird had flown against my window at home. I'd spotted it one morning when I was packing my swimming things; I'd just bought a new swimsuit in midnight blue and was not in the mood to fetch the rubber gloves and put the bird in the garbage. While I was swimming and later in the office, I had thought about it all the time. But when I'd come back that evening, it was gone. A cat must have come for it. To make sure it hadn't just dragged itself into some corner hidden from the living room, I went out onto the balcony—but there was nothing. I'd told Richard about the vanishing bird corpse. He'd just frowned and said that I shouldn't watch so many scary films. I pushed my hands deeper into my pockets. In the left one, I touched my key, in the right one, his: the choice was mine. This calmed me enough to face going back into the restaurant. At the table, it was obvious that I'd been away longer than I'd intended; the plates had been cleared away. The fact that I was hungry had hit me again outside on the empty street and I stared dumbly at the tablecloths of the best Thai place in Frankfurt. Rebecca's already paid, said Ines, adding, when I pulled out my purse, We're her guests. Carol and Rebecca's heads were huddled together like an undermanned team before a decisive match. Did I miss anything else? I whispered. Not much, Ines said, now we're going over to theirs to watch a film. I looked at her in horror but Ines just shrugged and remarked nebulously, It's Carol's evening. Outside, she had unlocked the car door and we were already sitting inside when Carol and Rebecca had a quiet, terse exchange of words. Then Rebecca turned and walked off briskly down the middle of the street. She stalked away across the glittering asphalt, brightly lit by street lamps, and her silhouette vanished into the darkness. She'd prefer to walk, said Carol as she climbed into the back and sat in the middle, thrusting her head between the seats to make sure we caught her every word. I realized that it hadn't been Rebecca's idea to watch a film; it had been Carol's. All her imaginary feelings were coated with her new love: an hour and a half in Ines' presence and she was as fragrant and dewy as freshly cut grass. She simply couldn't let go of her prize—and not even Rebecca, it seemed, had realized it was this bad.

Although the flat wasn't far from the restaurant and we had to go twice around the block until we found a parking space, Rebecca wasn't there when we arrived. The hallway of the apartment was as white as a doctor's surgery. The living room was white as well and next to white walls on white rugs stood white designer furniture. A white Persian cat sat proudly beneath a steel lamp that illuminated her with its cold light. All this reminded me of photographs in lifestyle magazines—except that the photographers normally went to great lengths to make sure that the places looked lived in. Nice, said Ines, and Carol basked in her compliment. It's Rebecca's flat, she said, she owns it. I only moved in a few weeks ago. I thought of Richard and his wife. How strange: people seemed to move swiftly in and out all over Frankfurt, first living together, then moving back to their own places. People in Rome were more sensible, prouder in this respect: they weren't as quick to leave or exchange the space they'd managed to inhabit. We sat down. Carol sank delightedly onto the sofa; Ines sat stiff and upright with a brooding expression. The cat looked longingly at her, then jumped onto a meticulously folded woollen blanket. Its white body formed a perfect circle. Smoking isn't allowed in here, is it? Ines reached out to touch the cat that stretched itself lengthways and then curled back up; its cathartic purring wasn't interrupted for the next quarter of an hour. Carol hesitated. Of course it is, wait a minute. She placed a strikingly ugly ashtray on the glass table, one of those metal devices that you rotated to make the ash fall down into the pot and hide the smell. This one was ugly but smaller than usual, about as big as an eggcup. On the spotlessly clean glass table, it looked like a giant wart. The cat pumped up its body again. Those are Rebecca's treasures, said Carol, indicating the sleek backs of the videotapes and DVDs that filled the wall cabinet. Nice, said Ines again. And because treasures are for admiring, I stood up and walked along the rows of films. Most of the titles didn't ring any bells but they did feature a whole bunch of dead people, revenants, werewolves, vampires and zombies. She also had all the classics, of course, including *Frankenstein* and *Frankenstein's Bride*, which made me think how I would have preferred to be with Richard tonight. Rebecca had noted the names of the directors and production years in capital letters on white paper sleeves if the films were missing their original cases. This gave her archive the neutral look of a patient's card index. The cat's called Romy, said Carol. She loves watching television. If we don't stop her, she sits on the set and hangs her head down like a bat. All three of us looked at Romy, who in turn was staring at Ines with her hypnotic eyes. There was a noise in the hallway and then Rebecca appeared with flushed cheeks. My eyes met hers in cool, flickering acknowledgement. Very refreshing, such a walk. Have you been here long? She said this in a slightly ironic tone as if making fun of herself; Carol and Ines shook their heads mutely in unison. I looked at Ines. There was something about her expression that made me break up the whole situation once and for all. It made me stand up and say, Sorry, I won't be sticking around for the film. I have a terrible headache all of a sudden. Ines can stay if she likes. But it'd be nice if she could drive me home first. I wasn't out to save Ines—I still hadn't warmed to her enough for that; I just wanted to destroy a game in which I felt she had the weakest role. Carol's face went slack as she said in a reproachful tone: But I've rented out comedies—comedies, not horror films. Ines, however, had already stood up and walked a few steps towards the coat stand in the hallway. Carol watched her go like a child whose favourite toy has suddenly grown legs just so it can leave its owner.

That was awkward, I said in the car, which Ines drove very slowly and carefully like a different person. Who on earth watches horror films as a job—of their own free will? Oh, she said, I'm sure it can be great fun. Yeah, sure, but that's not why she does it, I said, she's dead serious about it. She's fascinated by it because she's evil inside. I was talking rubbish, there was no doubt about it; in truth I was furious with Ines. I felt betrayed by her. I'd only wanted to show I was on her side—but her side was hers alone. Are you always so quick to judge people you've only just met? she went on to ask. Perhaps it's not like that at all. Perhaps it's a way for her to face her darkest fears. The exhaustion in her voice stopped me from making a sharp retort. I left it, saying that whatever the case, I found the pair of them totally obnoxious, and my tone said that the conversation was over. For the rest of the drive home, I let the street lights blur in front of my half-closed eyes. I became more and more frustrated. My frustration grew so much that I asked Ines to come up to my flat for a while to talk. She politely refused. Are you OK? You're so quiet, I insisted and she suddenly took my hand and said, Don't worry, of course. Then I started again, unable to contain myself: I don't understand why Carol had to show you off like that. Or why she just stood there and didn't do anything when Rebecca was being so rude. You know, said Ines, and looked at her hands resting on the steering wheel, clad in sand-coloured leather gloves. I hurt her very badly once and that was her revenge, setting Rebecca on me like that. That's how things go sometimes. Just an unhappy love story. I was drunk and she's waited a long time to pay me back. I guess you have to hand her this victory. Then she let me out and started up the engine before racing down the deserted street like a mad thing.

That was what puzzled me most of all: her sudden haste. That was why I couldn't relax at home, had to put on my coat and scarf after a quarter of an hour and go out again. I just wanted to see if her lights were out and she was asleep—if so, everything was fine. The streets were empty, the lamps lit up small pools; I walked through the back roads. A woman was leading a child by the hand on roller skates; the child was so tired that she lurched and threatened to fall over at any moment. I would have liked to have stopped them and asked what on earth a child of that age was doing on the street at that time of night. And on roller skates. But I went past them without uttering a word. The illuminated window of a bookshop caught my attention, but no sooner had I stopped in front of it than I thought I heard footsteps, got scared and turned into a main street. At Eschenheim Green, I crossed the city ring road which was only dotted with a couple of cars, and then it took me about fifteen minutes to reach Glauburgstrasse where Ines lived. I rubbed my cold hands and counted the storeys; no doubt about it, all the lights on the third floor were on. I wondered whether Kai might be there and if I would disturb them, then rang the doorbell.

She opened the door just a crack, her black dress matching the dark background of the hallway, making her white face look like a lantern hanging in the dark. She said, oh hello, without recognizing me straight away. Her eyes looked different—bigger, glittering and moist—and she seemed neither surprised nor disturbed that I was there. I was simply there, at her front door. and she opened it to let me in. Everything OK? I asked. Come in, she said, I'm just having a drink. Do you want a drink too, let's talk, shall we? She was in strangely high spirits, as if she was having a party all by herself. She spoke with strange clarity, pronouncing each word without paying attention to its place in the sentence, so that what she said was a random chain of words, spoken for the sake of speaking, as if she were sitting alone in a big field and the wind was tearing each one away. She seemed to have forgotten that we'd only just said goodbye, and greeted me as if we hadn't seen each other for months. Let's go into the living room, she said. She flounced through the sparse hallway from where I could see the brightly lit lounge. I stopped briefly in front of her bedroom. Something

had changed: it wasn't as empty as recently. A sea of
paper handkerchiefs, Coke cans and chocolate-bar
wrappers looked back at me in mute accusation;
among some old newspapers, the necks of two bottles rose up like lighthouses. On the pillows lay a
squashed teddy bear that seemed familiar. Are you
coming? she chirped, then followed my gaze and saw
what I saw. But instead of apologizing for the mess,
she ran past me to catch up the teddy in her arms:
Sebastian! Do you remember? And the way she stood
there, eager joy in her eyes, her hips thrust forward
in her dirty jeans—sassy, a touch lascivious—I forgot
time. I saw her as I'd often seen her when she was
ten or eleven: in her patterned pyjamas, not wanting
to go to bed, not wanting to sacrifice even the tiniest
bit of her day. I wanted to react, to say something,
to take her toy away, but I couldn't. I stood in the
doorway, frozen by sadness. Ines came out of the
pose, laughing and throwing the stuffed animal onto
the bed where the bear came to rest in a precarious
position, face down between a pillow and a knocked-
over bottle; then she walked past me back into the
kitchen, but not without throwing me a sidelong
glance as if to say, really, you're not the life and soul
of the party tonight. Come on, she trilled. I followed
her tiny, jeans-clad bottom. In the kitchen, a small
light was on above the sink. Ice? She led me into the
living room and sat down, cross-legged, on the sofa.
Her body was reflected in the flat blackness of the

silent TV. I sipped my Martini. Ines watched me. Not bad, huh? I just bought it at the kiosk. Talking of kiosks . . . she winked. Do you know what happens to me every evening, no matter what time I go out to buy some drink? There's always an old woman in dark clothes standing at the lamp post on the corner. She turns and faces me, following me with her eyes as I walk past. She's always wearing the same black raincoat and has a brown, folded-up umbrella in her hand. I've seen her on so many evenings, one after the other, and I've always wanted to ask her if she's looking for someone, or needs some kind of help; but something stops me. It's like—she broke off and started again—I'm afraid of her. She paused to take a drink. Every time, I swear I'll go a different way to the kiosk, or over to the all-night petrol station on Friedberger. But I never do. I'm always in a hurry and take the quickest route, whether I'm scared or not. I thought about the old woman Kai had photographed whose name I didn't know. Perhaps she's from the old people's home, the one on Grüneburg Park, I suggested, there's one there, you know? She's probably just out for a walk. Old people need much less sleep. No. Ines sounded impatient, No, you don't get it—*you* wouldn't see her. She doesn't exist, I'm the only one who can see her: she's death—my death. She poured herself more drink. I checked her face for signs that she was teasing me, or that satisfied expression I thought I'd seen when she was asleep. But I found nothing. She talked about herself like someone she didn't care for whatsoever. The ice in her glass clinked softly; she drank so quickly that the cubes barely melted and would do for another drink. There's a certain point you reach when you drink, she said pouring herself yet another: Something changes. Colours are different, smells are different, the way bodies expand in space is—how can I put it—more beautiful, alien, like in a parallel, better universe. Her collarbone trembled; she breathed deeply in and out, as if doing a yoga class. I slammed down my glass on her dirty table. There's only one thing I understand. You should stop drinking. Bodies expand in space when you're sober too. You'd know that if you just tidied this place up a bit. It was the only thing I could think of. I picked up the bottle but that didn't help; I didn't know where to go with it. Ines smiled. What music shall I put on? Leonard Cohen? I'm in the mood. Listen, I said, not taking any notice of her. You need help.

You need help, I said, and immediately realized that it wasn't the right direction to take things. Her mood changed as fast as a traffic light from green to red. Don't take that tone with me, she snapped. No one can cure me—I've tried explaining that to Kai too. Everyone's always trying but I'm going to stay the way I am. She wiped her nose on the sleeve of her sweatshirt. I'm going to stay the way I am, she repeated when I didn't react. She leant back on the sofa. I wasn't sure whether my being there was doing her good or simply pushing her further into the depths of misery. Surely she had to feel shame or something? But you're asking me for help, at least indirectly, I objected, still trying to have a normal conversation with her. She looked at me uncomprehendingly: A-ha. And I thought you'd come to visit me because you wanted to. But you're just another one with helper syndrome. I sighed. I'm worried. Surely you can understand that. Her only reaction was to stand up and slouch out of the room. Again I wondered whether she was working at all. Are you painting any more? Where are you going? I called after her, jumping up as well; it was like in Tom and Jerry. She had disappeared into the bathroom. I rattled the door but it remained locked. I spoke to the door: The only reason I came to see you was to say that if you need help . . . well, what I just told you. Was she trying to kill herself in there? It was more likely that she was looking at her pretty face in the mirror, feeling like the queen of the universe. The way she'd been prancing around before, in her alcohol buzz! I went into the hallway to get my jacket and then she came out. I was right: she had put on some make-up. There was much-too-thick eyeliner under her left eye. You don't understand me, she said stubbornly and stomped past me into the living room, her chin stuck in the air: you have no idea what I'm going through. I'll tell you what I do know, I explained. Addiction is a decision—no one's forcing you to do it. What you have to do now, Ines, is fight. While I was saying this, she looked at me with an unwavering stare that implied I was suggesting she should jump out of the window. I could sense her fear so palpably that it was like a third person in the room. In a flash, I realized that her mood was about to tip, any minute now. I remembered what Kai had said about this moment: she could become a danger to herself and others. I had to phone him. Ines? I asked. Where's your phone? She didn't reply but simply sniffed into her sleeve and pulled a scornful face, but I found her mobile anyway and tried to call up her contacts: there he was, thank God. Kai, I shouted, and he knew straight away that it wasn't good news. Where are you? he asked. At Ines' place, I answered. I see, he said slowly. How tedious this must be for him, hearing the same news over and over again. Ines bawled something in the background. I'll be over in a minute, said Kai and hung up. Ines was no longer in the living room but the bedroom door was now closed. Locked. I thought I could see her silhouette through the keyhole. She was sitting on her squalid bed, not doing anything, or so it looked. I stopped calling out to her and decided to wait for Kai. It suddenly hit me how exhausted I was. It's not the difference between dark and light but the difference between not living and being born at last! I heard her yell and then it all went quiet again.

Whatever! I shouted back. Worn out, I went into the bathroom where I splashed cold water on my face and combed my hair. Then I noticed the smell. I opened the toilet lid and saw traces of vomit. A saying went through my head: The really interesting things take place on the boundaries of good taste. Where the hell had I picked that up? It wasn't true anyway. I left the bathroom as it was and went back into the living room where I turned on the TV. The late-night news was on. A young woman had given birth to nine children and suffocated each one immediately after the birth. I fell asleep.

I must have at least nodded off when I was awoken by Kai's low, irritable voice and then Ines, who replied in that plaintive tone of hers I knew only too well. I listened while I took in where I was and what had happened. Kai must have his own key—in any case, I hadn't heard the doorbell. Then a door slammed, I sat up and he was standing in front of me. She's woken up and started drinking again, he announced. She'll fall asleep again soon. He took off his coat, and I thought he looked unnatural, like a bat that had shed its skin—and then I realized I had only ever seen him in his coat or in the dark at the shoot. He folded his coat with a forceful gesture and laid it on the sofa next to me. Underneath he was wearing an elegant suit that made him look older. How long has this been going on? I asked and crossed my legs as if we were experts having a talk. Three or four days, he said. Or perhaps a week? Yes, more like a week. I looked at him, aghast. You haven't seen her for a week? You knew that she was living like this and you left her on her own? I stared at him. He folded his coat in a different way and asked, Yes, so? She abases herself in many ways— most of it is sheer egotism and aggression. Before she met me, she coped, and before she met Carol or you, she always managed to make it home alone, don't forget that. But once you're in her force field, she won't let you go. She shackles you to her with that sick energy of hers—He abruptly broke off, dropping the sleeve he'd been lifting and talking to the whole time, pulling a face as if he'd expected more from this promising fabric. He sat down and stood up again. I have the impression she's getting worse, and the more understanding I show, the more she goes downhill. At first she just lay in bed on her days off and drank, thought she was adorable, didn't eat, only drank. It didn't affect her looks and on Monday morning, she'd cycle off to her studio in a good mood. But now? She doesn't even have a studio, I stated plainly. He didn't respond. Do you know what a home delivery is? I shook my head, not having the faintest idea, and so he told me: Some alcoholics live in places where there's nowhere to buy late-night booze, like the countryside or the suburbs, and so they phone a taxi and ask the driver to pick some up at the nearest all-night station. All they have to do is put a basket with a shopping list and money for booze and petrol in front of the door. Why are you telling me this? I asked airily, and Kai, sure of his punchline, replied: You asked me how we met. Well, that was the party. I looked at him more closely. You temped as a taxi driver? Only a few years ago?

Exactly, he answered, with slight impatience, and she asked me to run errands for her every night. Isn't that very expensive? Kai now threw me a scornful look and ignored the question. I'd never have met her if I hadn't waited one night at the front door to see who would collect the basket. It was just ugly old nosiness on my part. I wanted to see some hag gone to rack and ruin, or perhaps a granddad with his flies open. Christ, did I get a shock when I saw Ines—so young, at rock bottom. Oh yes, he said, getting worked up, I was shocked and I fell in love with her the minute I set eyes on her. Or at least I wanted to save her—an urge I confused with love for a long time. I got it all wrong. She used to be a great temptress. You should have seen her 'Moses Act' as I called it when she turned up at art shows back then—she'd walk slowly, dressed in immaculate outfits, and the crowd would draw back like the parting of the Red Sea. He began pacing again like he'd done recently. It was like sitting in the cage of a familiar hamster. I'll leave you two alone now, I said. And at that very moment, there was an almighty crash.

She was lying on the kitchen floor with her eyes open and although her mouth wasn't moving, she was making a whimpering sound. The puddle she was lying in reeked of booze; a chair had fallen over and the top door of the kitchen unit was open. There was blood on her hands and face. Her left leg was stretched out, the right one twisted into a bent position so that her heel was touching her bottom. I wanted to scream but then I held my hand in front of my mouth and knelt down to her. Only then did I notice the glass splinters. Careful, I said. Kai felt her pulse and talked to her the whole time: Everything's going to be all right, everything's going to be all right. Can you move this? No? Doesn't matter. Can you please phone an ambulance? he instructed me. And bring a pillow. We cushioned her to make her more comfortable, as far as this was possible without moving her leg. I fetched toilet paper and gently wiped her face. She wasn't injured there: the blood was coming from her hands and she'd wiped them across her face. No cuts there. I was relieved. I started cleaning up the splinters and liquid. It stank over-poweringly of strong spirits.

Kai held her hand, stroking it carefully so as not to move the improvised bandage I'd put on her cut. I stood next to the kitchen chair that we'd set upright, unable to grasp what had just taken place. We'd been in the room next door—how could this have happened? Why hadn't I just left instead of talking to Kai? What was I doing here if I was no help at all? Why hadn't I asked a doctor or a psychologist for advice weeks ago when I'd heard about her problem? The doorbell rang and I went to open it. The paramedics brought in a light stretcher which they laid Ines on after giving her an injection. I began to cry soundlessly but, as if he'd heard me, one of the paramedics turned round and said: It's probably not too bad, a thighbone fracture. Well, and the cuts, of course. Was she holding a glass when she fell? A really nasty fall. Only one of the two paramedics spoke while the other grimly carried out his work, glancing up now and again with a contemptuous look on his face. I felt as if the whole thing was a role play, like a good-cop/bad-cop thriller transposed onto the rescue services. Kai spoke quietly to the good one; I just carried on crying. There was nothing else I could do. He let them go on ahead and turned round to me. I'm going to drive to the hospital, he said, stretching out his hand to wipe a tear from my cheek with the tip of his finger. I'll phone you tomorrow. I thought I saw him lick the tear from his finger but I might have been mistaken—he may have just wiped his hand across his face. Still, when I saw that gesture which was meant for me and which I understood, I felt the first pang of guilt; and I knew that whatever happened from then on, I couldn't just be an observer. Perhaps it's not the worst thing that could've happened, said Kai. Then he rushed out after the paramedics and thundered down the stairs.

That had happened twelve hours ago—and now Richard was sitting in his baronial dressing gown in front of me, delighted that I was asking for his advice, thinking it over and not ready to give his verdict too quickly. He stretched out his naked, hairy calves, his feet perfunctorily clad in leather slippers which resembled the white ones supplied by hotels all over the world and which gave his feet just as little support. On the breakfast table in front of us were empty coffee cups, croissant crumbs, eggshells and a fruit bowl of grapes, bananas and apples as well as a cigarette lighter which had somehow ended up among them. I looked at this pile of objects, lying together yet contradicting itself, and compared the shiny red lighter to the shiny red apples—an opulent, Baroque still-life that made me introspective. Nothing was true unless it referred to something else. What I don't understand, said Richard, summarizing, is that you say she climbed up on a chair to fetch a bottle. Why the devil didn't she keep the bottle on the floor within reach? I took the lighter out of the fruit bowl and flicked it. I have a theory about that, I said, looking at the blue flame. Perhaps it sounds weird. When we were kids, Mum always hid sweets from us. She'd put them high up on the shelves, you know, so that we couldn't reach them. Richard, looking for cigarettes, patted the pockets of his dressing gown, an item of clothing that he liked to keep on until lunchtime at weekends. He offered me one but I shook my head. I see, he said, and leant in for a light.

Yes, that might be it. What hospital is she in? The Red Cross Clinic? Yes, right next to the zoo, I said. Perhaps you should talk to the doctor again. Tell him why she fell off the kitchen chair. Hmm, what else can you do? He puffed on his cigarette, creating the impression that the idea he'd just come up with was evaporating into thin air before he'd properly thought it over. I let him think some more and went into the bathroom where I looked at my face in the mirror. Since turning thirty, I'd imagined myself withering a little each day; now too, my appearance made me feel close to hysteria. I went nearer to the mirror before it completely misted up with my breath, then pulled away and began applying anti-ageing cream, this time my own because the cosmetics had disappeared from the shelf—out of the blue and much to my regret. In the empty space where they had been now stood my toothbrush and face cream, looking pretty lost.

We spent Sunday morning reading. I browsed through a new exhibition flyer but soon put it aside—all I could think of was Ines. I had plenty of questions and was slowly realizing that many of the answers I thought I had would need rethinking so that I could get to the bottom of the problem. Later on, Richard challenged me to a game of chess; although he tried to let me win, I still didn't. Even later on, we went out and when we came back, Richard suddenly tried to repair the hi-fi that had been broken for weeks. Do you have to do that now? I asked and he said, Yes, otherwise it won't leave me in peace. I knew exactly what he meant.

That evening, I went over to the window. Dusk had fallen and the world outside was made up of different hues of grey. Suddenly I forgot how my life had felt up until then—whether it had been good or bad. Suddenly, I felt as if I didn't have a body and was at one with the night, without contours, hardly weighing a thing.

On the way to the hospital, I could hear the zoo animals screeching, cawing and bleating; but as soon as I walked through the revolving door into the foyer, there was silence. The woman at the reception smiled and answered, Ms Franzen is in Room 311; then she carried on filling in a list. I walked noiselessly along the corridor that smelt of disinfectant and camomile, slowing down as I did. The sterile smell reminded me of a meeting I'd had with the estate agent who'd found me my current flat. But first she'd taken me to a place with a garden and I couldn't shake off the impression that she hadn't wanted to rent it out, not to me. We were standing on the veranda and I was looking at the ants on the tiles that were scurrying about in the autumn sun. The estate agent pulled a despairing face and said, yes, they eat everything—

leaves, cables, even plasterwork. She gave me a look of strained self-control as if she was about to collapse; I didn't say anything, not having any tips on pest control. Well, she said, pulling herself together again, it's really difficult to get rid of them. But the ant problem hadn't bothered me because I hadn't wanted a ground-floor flat anyway.

Ines was lying in a two-person ward; the bed next to hers was empty and messy. Hello, she said, her head pressed into her pillow. Her left leg was in a cast and was hanging by an apparatus in a raised position. Nice of you to come. Her lips were bluish, her gaze weak: it could have been the face of a dying woman. You look good, I said. She shrugged, causing the bedclothes to slip off her shoulders. She had on a white shirt which made her skin look even more pallid. I sat down on the edge of her bed, setting my rucksack on the floor. The present inside didn't go together in the least with what I was about to say. Ines, I said, beginning my awkward, impossible, ridiculous lecture, you'll see that there are other things besides this sickness. I went on in this vein: I talked, she nodded, half-amused, mockingly, as if I were saying exactly what she had expected me to say, which was probably true. But I had something different in store. I've brought you a present, I said, with an enigmatic smile. If you need a vase, she said, sounding infinitely exhausted and fed up, you'll have to ring for the nurse. I shook my head; no, I didn't have flowers in my rucksack. I lifted up my bag and let her peer inside. She laughed out loud. What the hell? Her eyes narrowed into suspicious slits; she couldn't believe it, and right then nor could I. I tried to remember what had made me go into that fancy whisky shop to buy the bottle: a good, expensive brand. I had wanted to lend the whole business a kind of dignity. I said, well, I guess it'll be tough on you to go cold turkey and I don't want you to have to ask another patient. That's why. Anyway, you know you have to get professional help and give up completely—very soon. As I was saying this, I had unwrapped the bottle and set it on the bedside table where its golden, shiny body radiated self-assurance. I stroked the cool glass. What I didn't say to her was that I didn't want her to sink any lower. She nodded. It was a good thing that she didn't seem too pleased—then I would have thought I'd made a mistake. Take my toothbrush mug, it's above the sink. Pour me some, please. I passed her the mug, filled halfway. And she drank the way I'd often seen her drink; and I was sure I'd be able to spot an alcoholic at the first sip from then on. Her face turned a more natural colour, as if I'd given her medicine. Her eyes glistened as if she'd undergone a miraculous cure. Poison and medicine, the same substances—it only came down to the dosage. Do you really think Kai would leave you? I asked out of the blue. Strange, I became talkative when she drank. She nodded. When I feel better, yes. Right now, he daren't. I was surprised at her answer and pressed her, and she said, you heard right. He's weak. He'll find another sick woman who needs his help and whose suffering he can work on. But if he doesn't, it won't be his fault. She spoke in a dull, grumpy tone that I ought to have found unpleasant, but I didn't. Why? I thought of Father and his bleak speeches, and how I used to imagine I was the only one who understood him. I looked uneasily around at the white hospital room. My gaze fixed on the neighbour's unmade bed. At the foot lay a brown-grey, musty-looking woollen pullover that probably smelt of dogs or horses or both. Talking of Kai, said Ines. He has a lot on his plate at the moment, which is why I don't want to bother him. Could you fetch me a few things from my flat? Some books, a couple of T-shirts, shampoo, that kind of thing? She reached out for a pen and paper from her bedside-table drawer. I'll note down where you can find everything. On the desk in the study, there's a plastic bag from the bookshop with thrillers inside. Funny, I'd just bought them. As if I knew. She laughed drily, a laugh that turned into a cough. There's a plant in the kitchen. If it's already dead, throw it away. Otherwise there's a watering can in the bathroom. She made notes, her lips shining moistly while her hair fell across her chest onto the paper; she brushed it away impatiently. What she said about the plant made me sad; my sister clearly cared as little for her things as she cared for herself. I decided to water the plant, no matter what. Voilà. She passed me the sheet of paper. My door key must be in my coat pocket. I obediently stood up and went over to the wardrobe. At that moment, the door opened and in came a plaster-cast arm. It was followed by the head of a woman with short brown hair: one eye was infected and red. Oh, the woman said in a high, disappointed tone, eyeing me suspiciously, you have a visitor, and Ines said, Yes, you missed her, whereupon the whole woman slid into the room. She had a tote bag cleverly slung over her cast, from which peeked a sheaf of magazines. When she reached her bed, she unhooked the bag with her intact arm. Got them all for free. Didn't buy a single one. She swelled with pride. When I'm done with them, you can have 'em all. No need, said Ines, my sister just promised to fetch some things for me. Your sister. That's you? The woman inspected me. It seemed that she was overfamiliar with everyone but introduced herself to no one. I nodded coolly; this roommate would have rustled up a bottle for Ines only too gladly, as long as she was allowed to keep the change. In that respect, I'd made the right decision. The woman fell noisily onto her bed and with a loud rustling sound, started arranging her looted magazines around her like an elaborate nest. But instead of opening one, she picked up her hairbrush and groomed her short hair while gazing at us with a vacant look. Next to the pristine bed sheets, the whites of her eyes looked yellowish. She wasn't the kind of person who wanted to talk, it seemed: she preferred eavesdropping. I picked up my empty rucksack and went over to Ines. For the first time in a long time, I hugged her as we said goodbye.

In the zoo, only a few visitors were dotted about. Stray beams of light fell on the narrow paths. Every few yards I stopped mechanically in front of a cage or enclosure and looked in. Many were empty; it was probably too cold. Two bored-looking bears sat in front of a rock. A dromedary came over to the fence where I was standing. Lamas, goats, ponies, wild boars. From one of the aviaries came a loud screeching noise—glancing inside I saw cockatoos, canary birds and macaws showing off their strawberry-red and bright green plumage. In a long, low pen whose fence only reached to my waist, a huddle of guinea pigs was tussling over lettuce leaves. Each one that wasn't shoved aside by others ate with the uniformity of a hunched, savage little machine. But the lettuce did not appear to get any less, because as soon as they grabbed one leaf, another tumbled out of the feeder. The longer I watched them and the more details I noticed about these tiny creatures, the more monstrous they seemed.

I soon lost interest and went past the big cat pen towards the exit. Dusk was falling. In the aviary, the lights flickered on. Faintly phosphorescent, grey-violet shadows flitted across the deserted seal and penguin pools. My steps crunched on the gravel as I walked towards the revolving door. I hadn't yet discovered what kind of animal had screeched so loudly earlier on.

Back home, I unlocked the entrance door to the flats and went into the hallway, triggering the automatic neon light. I blinked. On the bottom step was an Argos catalogue with someone else's address on it. I took it up to my flat, whumped it on the desk and began skimming through the index: *Accessories, Action figures, Art supplies* . . . There it was, on page 1,276—the professional easel that Ines had been given on her thirteenth birthday. It took up half of the left-hand page. In front of it stood a button-down, blonde model in a white shirt, holding a brush and palette in her hand as if they were alien objects, as if she'd just found them on the street and wasn't really sure what these strange implements were for. I carefully tore out the page. Then I paced the living room before walking into the kitchen where I tore open a free-sample packet of crisps. I walked around, dropping bits on the parquet floor.

The books were in the study, Ines had said. If I'd imagined something like Bluebeard's Chamber, then

I was disappointed. There was a desk, empty except for the plastic bag she'd mentioned with the books inside and a cork board decorated with two rows of drawing pins. Two Post-its were stuck on the bare wall; on one was my telephone number. In the wastepaper basket lay a few crumpled sheets that I carefully fished out and smoothed flat. They were covered with sketches and squares, lines connected by single words; the handwriting was untidy and smudged and there were underlinings and crossings out with stick men scurrying all about, strange stars and a dozen other mysterious ciphers. I also found a few photocopies from an art-history book with illustrations of various gods. I looked at pictures of Apollo and read the caption: *Apollo, ruler of the spheres and ruler of time, depicted with the Muses, planets and the Three Graces.* The three animal heads of the serpent represented the three aspects of time: the lion symbolized the present, the wolf the past and the dog the future. I stood there for a long time, looking at the pictures, thinking about what Kai had said. There were several loose-leaf binders in her desk drawer. I quickly flicked through the first: bank statements, bills, a six-month-old termination notice for a flat in Glauburgstrasse, which must have been Ines' studio. I put the file back and closed the drawer. I took the plastic bag and was about to go when I heard a noise: a deep, elderly voice was talking in the living room. I stopped, fear stealing through me.

But the intruder was talking about renewed icy temperatures. Despite this, I bent down and took my boots off before tiptoeing into the next room where the TV screen gave the darkness a bluish hue. The weatherman disappeared and film music started up. I sank onto the sofa in relief, gazed at the ghostly TV and breathed in and out deeply for a few seconds. It was hot in the flat, I now noticed, and, although I had slipped off my shoes, I was still wearing my coat as I'd been in a hurry to get to the study. I pulled off the jumper I was wearing over my shirt and left it lying on the sofa.

I went into the bathroom and drew myself up in front of the mirror. The neon strip along the top of the mirror cabinet tinged my face a greenish yellow. I was wearing a crumpled shirt, a skirt and tights. Slowly, I took off one thing after the other except for my underwear, all the time keeping my eyes on the green pall of my face. Then I turned away from this ridiculous sight and padded about barefoot. The edges of the bathtub gleamed, towels hung untidily on the rails, a dressing gown lay on the floor. Ines' underwear was hanging to dry over the white radiator; black panties and bras whose straps dangled like spiders' legs. I fingered a particularly pretty set: black, tiny flowers made of lace with eggshell-coloured cups shimmering through. It was dry. I pulled off my things and put on hers. They fitted. I pulled my hair back and twisted it into a loose ponytail, the way

Ines did sometimes, fixing it with a rubber band that I found on the edge of the sink. Then I sat down on the edge of the bath to think.

From the TV next door, dramatic, sentimental music could be heard, and then an authoritative voice said something that I couldn't understand. Still sitting on the edge of the bathtub, I pulled up the lace of the bra, stuck a finger under the left cup and began to trace the tip of my breast. I leant forward a little so that I couldn't see anything except the lemon-coloured, unvarying tiles, and thought about the men I'd slept with so far. All of them, except for Richard, had been fairly old. Because when I'd gone to Rome to study art history, a cultured gerontophilia had been in fashion that favoured forty- to sixty-year-olds, as opposed to my peers, who looked like parrots with their green-and-orange dyed hair.

I heard a key in the door, footsteps and then Kai walked down the hallway. First he walked past the bathroom, then came back and we stared at each other for a second, speechless. Without taking his eyes off me, he said that he had come back to turn off the TV. That's good, I said, it's still on, and together we listened. Screams could be heard, fire-engine and police-car sirens, women shrieking, children bawling—all the acoustic banalities of an action film. And then, as if it were part of the film, Kai took a step towards me, a wildly resolute look on his face, took my wrist and pulled me up from the edge of the

bath. I stared at him in astonishment. For a second I
felt like I was hovering in the air, and the last images
I'd taken in flashed through my mind—the lemon-
coloured tiles, an unvarnished big toenail, the tip of
a shoe. Three random things among many others in
the room that had etched themselves onto my mind
to form a still life, and which belonged together for
ever more. They were trivial but, at that moment,
they took on a huge significance. As Kai lifted me up
and carried me into the living room, it went through
my mind that a similar series of random things could
be brought together in any situation; I saw the
opportunity I had almost given up on: to piece my
life together—which until now had seemed to be a
loose, unrelated series of events—and form some
kind of whole.

In the living room, Kai went over to the TV with
me in his arms, and, squatting in an athletic but not
effortless way, turned it off with the tip of his shoe.
Once in the living room, his eyes scanned this all-too-
familiar place as he looked for a spot without a story,
a place where he could set me down. He hesitated,
took a step forward and then one back; the playful,
erotic situation of just a few minutes earlier became
precarious and threatened to tip. I was already stiff-
ening in his arms and he felt it, so out of helplessness and a lack of alternative he decided that we
were going to make love on the floor. He didn't put
me down but let us sink together, kneeling while

still holding me in his arms. He swayed, and I was thrown against him. I tried to adjust all my weight and rest only on his shoulders to give him a stable centre of gravity; I flung my arms around his neck and laid my head on his chest. We got closer to the floor where I instantly raised my head to kiss him. As we kissed, we both lay down, stretched out, faced each other in an undecided position on the floor, our bodies lit by a dim lamp next to the sofa. Then he pulled his lips away from mine to sit halfway up and slip off his clothes. I didn't help; I just watched, and as he took off his watch, a dog began to bark in the flat above us. It was a desolate yapping, a cascade with no let-up. It even carried on when I was stroking Kai's back, his ribs, his waist and his hips. At some point I didn't hear it any more because we were panting too loudly and my ears began to buzz as if I were in too-deep water, plunging down to unfamiliar depths but not afraid.

I was soon oblivious to our surroundings and the room was indifferent to us; I sensed the expressionless, rigid gaze of the walls that no longer delimited the boundaries of a flat but simply provided the setting for an ancient ritual. We didn't get tired or perhaps we just didn't want to stop so that we wouldn't have to think, or let our passion fade to memory—who believes in memories of passion anyhow?—and we were thrown together and pulled apart by the force field between us, over and over again, until suddenly, as if we'd been abruptly switched off by an unknown force, we stopped. The dog was still yapping. We lay there, cheek to cheek, his hair in front of my eyes, my eyelids twitching. Looking up to one side, I saw his chest hair stuck together damply, and I thought: that didn't take long, it just seemed that way; it had been quick and intense with no let up. And it'd had little to do with tenderness, the way we had taken possession of each other.

No, it'd had nothing to do with tenderness, although strangely, I couldn't get that word out of my head. But now, as we lay tightly nestled together and all our nervousness had vanished, I imagined that there was room for that. I firmly believed it, just as— and this became clear to me for the first time—just as I'd believed from the very start that I could be the one who gave him peace: this incredible peace and satisfaction that now radiated from him as he lay there next to me, and which seemed to have nothing to do with knowledge or hope, but simply existed, obscure and heartbreaking, beyond time and place. Perhaps it was dispelled loneliness, forever-banished solitariness. There it is, said Kai, without warning, in a voice that sounded angry, that stupid dog again.

That stupid dog again, I repeated to myself, quietly and incredulously. He knew that dog, and not just the dog. He was absolutely familiar with the situation: he'd just slept with a woman and that dog was yapping—that stupid dog. It was a familiarity that hurt me so much—I was new to all this—that I started to cry. What's the matter? he asked looking concerned, almost crushed, and I asked him for a glass of water. He immediately peeled himself away from me and padded barefoot to the kitchen. When he came back, I was lying on the sofa, staring at the ceiling; I shifted a little to make room for him, then some more because he wanted to stretch out next to me, and that's how we lay, motionless, curled up, me lying in his arms, a silent madness driving me to carry on my noiseless crying.

When I woke up, I was confused at first. Most of the room lay in darkness and I cautiously lifted my head. On the coffee table next to the sofa stood two glasses of wine, as dark as lion's blood; one glass was half-empty, the other full. My gaze wandered across the room. Kai was sitting at the other end of the room at the dining table; he was dressed and working. In front of him lay files, pens and a tray with a cup and teapot. I could hear his only-just-audible breaths, which I found soothing.

Turning to look at me, Kai smiled, told me I'd slept fitfully and that he was hungry. Let's go and eat something, he suggested, there's a snack bar still open. What time is it? I wanted to know. Almost two, he replied, then, without waiting for my answer, he went into the bathroom and I heard water running. I went over to the dining table where he'd been sitting.

Pens and lots of negative files were lying about, and, on a white piece of paper, a selection of pictures: 35C, 26C, 19A . . . I lifted one of the neg sleeves and held it against the light of the desk lamp which he had been using to help him. I saw shampoo bottles and pictures of a landscape that I couldn't place, neither the region nor the season—it lay there as if slumbering. I leafed through the next folder, searching, and the next and that's when I found all the old people. I looked at the oval, round and square shapes of their faces: all their small wrinkles and furrows, the thin lines between their eyes, eyelids, lips and hair, tiny shadows. And then her—the old woman with a look of shining pain in her eyes. Kai had circled this photo, which I liked straight away, with a red felt-tip pen. 22D—that was her number.

We got dressed, I dallied; the flat key was already in my hand, but I stopped in the hallway instead of going to the door, causing Kai to grab my hand and pull me impatiently. But still I didn't move—I couldn't. I stood there for a few seconds, motionless like in a film still, paralysed by a grief that had suddenly overcome me. Kai let go of my hand and repeated that we had to leave now, otherwise he would die of hunger. I pointed to my rucksack that was lying in the hallway and said, And what about afterwards, I mean are we coming back? and he said, Yes, we can leave our things here. I bent down anyway and quickly took out my key, purse and notebook. We walked out into the night. I had to screw up my eyes because they started to tear from the cold and I breathed out, making a small cloud that sailed upwards. I followed it with my eyes, looking up at Ines' house where the windows were all dark except for one: we'd forgotten to turn off the lamp in the living room. We turned right and immediately spotted the snack bar on the corner of Glauburgstrasse. It was the only lit building in the area; everything else was dark, this was a residential area. We stepped out of the night and into the brutal efficiency of neon-strip lighting that leached the colour from everything in the room with its dazzling whiteness. The waitress, a young girl, looked like a ghost. We were the only guests. We sat down at a tiny table for two. The table was too close to the wall so Kai lifted it and pulled it away slightly. It was made of aluminium and didn't seem to weigh anything. I looked up—the big mirror on the longest side of the room reflected what he was doing. His face was white too. I quickly looked away again.

The waitress came over to our table, her arms swinging as if she were moving in time to some song in her head and having taken Kai's order, strolled away just as casually. I sometimes come here in the evenings, said Kai. I live in Westend. He opened a small matchbook. Siesmayerstrasse—d'you know it? Right by the Palmengarten. We should go for a walk there some time. He spoke and smoked with pleasure, and I was nervous and hoped that his relaxed mood would soon catch on. But for the time being, I let him do the talking. What I'd wanted to happen was happening—he was opening up. But I couldn't concentrate, which he soon noticed and so he drank his beer in silence. He had rolled up his shirtsleeves; I could read his watch. It was nearly three o'clock. Tomorrow in the office, Richard would ask why I was so bleary-eyed. The sandwich came and the waitress put it between us, giving us a paper napkin in which the knives and forks were wrapped. I touched the plastic, candy-coloured skewers that were stuck in the sandwich at regular intervals to hold it together. The body of Saint Sebastian, Kai remarked and twitched his knife. I started crying again. He squinted and said, is this a chronic thing? Do you always cry once or twice a day? No, I sobbed, no, wiping my hand across my face. A gust of cold air announced the arrival of other guests, clearly a couple, because they were holding hands. In their padded bomber jackets, baseball caps and short hair, the two of them looked so similar that only at second glance could I make out who was the man and who the woman. She was wearing court shoes and woollen leggings; he, trainers. After they came in, they immediately grabbed each other's hands again, as if there were a storm raging in the place and one of them might be whisked away. They sat down right next to us, although all the other places were free, and held hands across the table. The part of the duo that I presumed was the woman nodded encouragingly at my tearstained face, as if she wanted to say, a spat between lovers, understandable, a few coarse words and clichés at three in the morning—that's normal. She annoyed me. The pair of them loudly ordered champagne. How inappropriate in a place like this, I thought; but then my conversation with Flett Junior came to mind. Perhaps they were having the most romantic moment of their lives. Kai sawed away at the bread. Help yourself if you like, he said, and, struggling to suppress the impulse to stick out my tongue at the gawking woman waiting for her champagne, I grabbed the fork. The stupid thing fell on the floor and the clatter was incredibly loud. Whoops, I said, like a clown who'd just dropped her juggling balls. Immediately, the waitress came strolling over with a new set of cutlery wrapped in a serviette, which she waved in the air like a miniature walking stick. OK, said Kai and pulled his wallet out of his pocket, it's late. Let's grab a couple of hours' sleep. I looked at him calmly as he paid.

But the door had hardly shut behind us and we were standing on the deserted street when I started yelling at him, taking him completely by surprise. You can't do this, you can't just pretend this is normal, I said, and he, who had been about to put his arm around my shoulders, looked at me, first stunned, then defensively, even disgustedly. He took a few deep breaths before he spoke, and, when he did, he emphasized every word as if talking to an idiot. No, it's certainly not. I take all this seriously, so seriously, in fact, that I don't think we can straighten everything out tonight. As he was speaking, he'd taken a step back, balled his hands into fists and stretched his arms out slightly to his sides so that in silhouette, he looked like a rocket propped by its supports. You'll have to make a decision, I said, I hope you realize that, and he replied, What we did *is* a decision. For me or for her? I asked scornfully. I don't know, he said, no less angrily, not for her, by the look of it. We eyed each other for a while. I thought, he continued, you felt too that we should spend this evening, this *night*—he corrected himself—as if. As if, I repeated contemptuously and stamped my foot, but I was only putting on an act. I knew what he was trying to say; I'd already understood and was deliberately destroying it. He took a step towards me, and, taking my face in his hands, said, What should I have done? I don't know, I replied, I don't know what you should have done but it would be awful to think you can just forget Ines. No, he said, letting go of my face, I always see her when I look at you. There's a lot of you in her. I needed her in order to meet you, you see; she was your predecessor. No, I said, with icy calmness, I don't see, and I turned around and walked off in the opposite direction. He didn't stop me.

I spent the day at the newsroom in a state of complete exhaustion. In the afternoon, before it got busy, I quickly skimmed through other newspapers for subjects that might make good lifestyle stories. One, which certainly wasn't suitable, happened to catch my eye. A penguin had accidentally travelled halfway around the world. It had got caught in a Japanese fishing net and ended up in the refrigerated hold with all the fish. At temperatures of minus 20 degrees, the penguin had held out in its icy prison by living off the fish until it was discovered when the cargo was offloaded on the Canary Islands. Now it was recovering in Tenerife in one of the biggest penguin enclosures in the world. I looked at the photo next to the article: perhaps it would cheer up Ines. On the way home, I bought another bottle of whisky, had it gift-wrapped and sent to the hospital by courier. The salesman, whose elegant moustache bobbed when he stood on tiptoe to reach the upper shelves, waved after me when I left the shop. That'll make someone very happy, were his parting words, and I replied, No doubt about that. Happy just isn't the word.

As I'd expected, I ran into Kai that evening at Ines' flat. I tried to open the door quietly using the key— but obviously not quietly enough because I'd hardly set foot inside before he appeared. I knew you would come, he said triumphantly; you left your rucksack here. It was still lying next to the coat stand. I could have just taken it and left. It was nearly empty and from Kai's look, I knew that he knew. I took out all the important things yesterday, I said. The important things, I see, he said, and began unbuttoning my coat.

We were lying together and talking, trying to join up our two biographies. It was so dark in the room that I didn't even have to close my eyes to imagine what he was describing: starting with his life as a photography student, an observer of life, to the taxi driver who got to know Ines, he came full circle to the present. Only if we'd got up and looked at his circle from a distance, we might have noticed it wasn't complete. But this way, from our point of view in bed, it kind of was. Just as mine was, and our two complete circles—how could it have been otherwise—overlapped. The thought of this overlap, which existed because we'd found it, stirred our passion again. A more relaxed passion than the first time.

I talked about the things that had paralysed me, and about the dead time when I'd tried to become like Ines but she'd shown no interest in me whatsoever. I told him about the period when I was chubby and Ines was the princess, my princess, while I was just a nobody, no one special, and that the feeling hadn't gone away when I saw her these days. I don't think he understood everything but it didn't matter. I told him about the men in my life: my father, my marriage, that I was divorced—an Italian, a mistake, end of story. The fact that I'd let my husband do more with my body than I'd ever imagined possible. Is that so, said Kai, sitting up and leaning against the wall. Was there jealousy on his face? Yes, I said, that's so, and for a change, I accepted his offer of wine and cigarettes.

A scene in front of me, fleeting and flickering, like a passage from a dream. I try to grasp it and call up the whole episode in my mind. He could have been one of those actors who get up to all sorts in hospital soaps, the exotic, foreign type; his name, Dr Jadu, sounded foreign too. A suntanned, puffy face, held together by a smile. I'd hardly sat down in the waiting room when he said: You've come to see me? I had just turned sixteen. I had read that teenagers in America were doing it, and I wanted it done too, all at once, all the parts of my body listed under 'liposuction': thighs, waist, upper arms and so on. That morning, I had put on a particularly unflattering shirt and ugly stretch jeans. I wanted the surgeon to understand immediately why I was there. But he only looked into my eyes as if he wanted to climb in and operate on my soul. Well? He sent his receptionist out with a casual wave of his hand, which I was grateful for. Everything about him was laid-back: his white doctor's coat, with only one button done up, looking like he'd just thrown it on; his brown skin and dark eyes, which were rested as if he'd just come back from a golfing holiday or his private yacht. But the gigolo aspect of his appearance didn't fool me—

I'd done my research and called the Medical Association by pretending to be a journalist. He had an unusually high reputation. He was one of those clever people making money from a modern dream, and I was one of those dumb young things who wanted to let him. I stood up and quickly bared my arm, waving it in the air like a policewoman saying stop, and with my other hand, I squeezed the fleshy mass underneath. All this has to go, I said. Dr Jadu felt and tested it in the way our mother did when checking kiwis or avocados for ripeness, and I waited, as helpless as a piece of fruit, for the doctor's assessment. Well, he said, there's a problem. This here is flesh, not fat. We'd have to cut it away. He gazed at me intently with his brown eyes. Good, I agreed, then cut it away, and soon, I thought, he would pick up the long, horizontal diary from his desk and ask, OK, when were you thinking of? Before March if possible, I'd say with fake boredom. But it didn't happen that way. Instead, he sat on his stool and looked at me with a serious expression. Then he shook his head. What I mean is that you will be left with enormous scars—scars that will be obvious and ugly. I strongly advise you not to go ahead with this. But can it be done? I asked. By this time, I was sitting down again with my legs stretched out to the left and right. I'll tell you right now: plenty of my colleagues would do it without hesitation. Plenty of my colleagues would do many things without batting an eyelid. I felt a rush of hope. He saw it and sighed.

You're such a pretty girl. You don't know what you're talking about. Are you really eighteen? Doesn't matter. This here, he said tapping my thigh so that it gave me goose pimples, this is flesh. He spoke with an almost religious reverence. You must be able to see that—it's healthy flesh, be thankful. Do you know that most people I treat are accident victims? I don't believe that, I said stubbornly. The woman in the waiting room didn't look like one—more like a model. Well, he said angrily, whatever. I am not going to do it, and I'll tell you something. If you go ahead with this, you'll regret it for the rest of your life.

It was later than I'd intended, it was already five by the time I arrived at the hospital the next afternoon, murmuring an apology as I slipped off my parka. I'd already left my mark on it—I noticed a small rip in the sleeve as I hung it over the visitor's chair. I had put it on to please Ines but she didn't take any notice. I wasn't disappointed. Who knows, perhaps that hadn't even been the reason; perhaps in truth I'd just wanted to keep up the illusion that I could wiggle out of everything as easily as I could out of this coat. On the floor next to Ines' bed were two vases: a small one with a bunch of roses in it, and next to it, one with a colourful bouquet of chrysanthemums— purple, red and yellow, bright splashes of colour in the quiet whiteness of the room. Ines was lying against her pillows. What she'd been doing before I came wasn't clear; the TV was off and there was no book lying nearby. Her head seemed to have shrunk; it only took up the lower part of her pillow. She lifted it a little. There must be a lot to do at your office. Yes, of course, I said, impressed by her tone, which managed to sound both melancholy and accusing. She looked up at me, her eyes void of make-up. Out with it, she commanded. Like on my first visit, I opened my rucksack and lifted up the neck of the bottle. This time it was an eighteen-year-old Highland Park, achingly awaited by my beautiful sister, the boozer, who was lying in front of me. I swivelled my gaze over to the neighbour's bed. Ines' disagreeable roommate had her back to us and was pretending to be asleep. What about her? I whispered. It doesn't matter, said Ines in an exaggeratedly loud voice. She'd taken the bottle from me and, with one hand lying at an angle across her body, she nestled it in the bedclothes so that her other hand was free to stroke the smooth paper of the label, to run her hand up its glassy neck and then back to the label. She looked relaxed as she cradled and stroked the bottle, like a mother rocking her baby. I was embarrassed. What were you going to say just now? I asked. But Ines shook her head. Later. The glasses are over there. Reluctantly, she took one hand off the bottle and pointed to the sink. Next to the toothbrush mug were some glasses. I placed two on Ines' bedside table. Nice flowers, I said. She let out a *pfff* sound, giving the impression she'd never noticed any flowers. But she was enjoying the whisky. In the bed next to her there was still no movement, although the sleeping woman must have moved without me noticing because now a bush of hair was visible. The radiator gurgled. No sound from the street, but fast footsteps and excited voices went past in the corridor. That's better, said Ines. Another sip, the same phrase: that's better. She repeated it in a mindless kind of way. Yes, I said aggressively, we're all better. Ines leant back comfortably into her pillows. What I wanted to say is—they're letting me out in a week. And get this. I spoke to a nurse and they're going to get me a place at a clinic. You talked to a nurse? Really? I became very agitated. Actually, the nurse approached me, Ines corrected herself, and just imagine what she asked—whether I'd used alcohol to sterilize the holes in my earlobes. She'd always done that when she'd had an infection. Of course, I thought that she'd been nosing around in my bedside cabinet and knew everything. Afterwards, when I'd confessed, I realized that she was just naive. Earlobes, can you believe it.

I went over to the window that looked out onto the stone walls of the zoo. Visitors' cars were parked in front of them. A mother unfastened her daughter from a child seat and set her down on the street. The little girl looked out anxiously from under her woolly hat. I turned mechanically back to Ines. Where? I mean . . . There's a rehab clinic in Taunus, she said. I'll be going straight there when they discharge me. One of the doctors here has been very attentive. Her mischievous self-confidence flashed for a second; she fluttered her eyelids playfully and I laughed. I knew you wouldn't lose your knack for bewitching men that quickly. Isn't it wonderful? She drank and looked at me. After her fit of cheerfulness, her head had sunk back into the pillows and looked shrunken again, cushioned like a doll's head in a box. That's great, I murmured. I could hear my heart labouring, and felt a tingling in my shoulders. What would happen now? The door opened, and a bright voice sliced the room in two: Well, well, well, what do we have here, then? You girls painting the town red?

Carol's green coat was wide open, and no sooner had she walked through the door than she started making wild hand gestures to brush her red hair out of her face and describe the scene in front of her: she was delighted with herself for summing it up so perfectly. Bending over Ines, she pulled her into a hug, then plumped up her pillows and checked on the flowers. They're lasting well, she said, plucking off a bent leaf. But there are more popular presents, I can see, she grinned. A gust of her sickly perfume wafted towards me. She looked around but couldn't spot a second chair. In the next room a door slammed, and, as if I'd been given a secret cue, I stood up, grabbed my parka and rucksack and said, I'm out of here, this room feels crowded. But not because of me, surely, said Carol, immediately sitting down on the free chair. She practically took it away from beneath me so that the straps of my rucksack got caught on the armrest, and Carol nearly landed on the floor. This bovine burlesque set off explanations from Ines: You told me you were coming in your lunch hour, she said, that's why it suited me for Carol to come in the afternoon. Yes, I interrupted, blowing her a kiss. This time I didn't want to give her a hug, not in front of Carol. But I didn't want to storm out too quickly either; it wasn't like I was running away, which is why I moved slowly to the door and paused by the sink to fix my scarf, just for a moment; but Carol used it to turn quickly, chair and all, towards me. I'll be in the Orion tonight, she said looking up at me from an angle, her cherry-red lips glistening. Why don't you come? Yes, maybe, I said, making it sound like *no way*. Behind Carol, I saw Ines trying mutely to convey a message, pointing several times to the bottle and the wrist where she normally wore her watch. She nearly lost her cool because I, her pusher, didn't want to draw attention to her. She was on the brink of summoning me out loud to come again soon when I said, I'll come and visit you again really soon, Ines, I promise.

The sparkle of longing in Ines' eyes pursued me as I rushed down the white hospital corridors. What have

I done? I asked myself, not knowing whether I meant the bottle or the night before. I nodded to the nurse who was coming towards me down the corridor; I saw her elderly, benevolent face and was sure that she was the one who had talked to Ines. Later, without noticing, I walked through the zoo for who knows how long, holding up my weekly ticket to the man in the little cabin and walking past the enclosures—the big cat house, the aviaries, the lamas and seals. I pushed the revolving door at the exit and walked in the direction of Hanauer Landstrasse. I was freezing. I noticed a man watching me from the fast-food restaurant. He was sitting on one of those rows of stools with a view onto the street, not taking his eyes off me as he lit a cigarette. I suddenly wished I were invisible. I stopped the next taxi. The Orion, please. Such a long way? That's really worth my while, said the driver disparagingly. I couldn't see his hair or neck because he was wearing a scarf and woolly hat. I could only see his reddish face and squinting eyes in the rear-view mirror; his bushy eyebrows gave him a demonic air. First he drove carefully, as if I were made of porcelain, then suddenly sped up. I pressed myself into the backrest of the seat and regretted not walking. I looked out of the window, unsure whether the driver was taking a detour; in any case, there was the long wall of the zoo again, red brick—it could have easily been a cemetery wall—which turned into one long, grey-red blur when the driver put his foot down. Not a minute later, he braked sharply. There you go, he said. I stumbled to the entrance. The light was colder this time, or at least that's how it felt. As I came in, it lit too sharply the worn-out faces of the three women sitting at the bar, who were having an animated conversation behind tall glasses. But those three weren't the only guests. Hello, called a voice behind me, much too shrill for my liking. The three women fell silent, looked around and then began talking again, now more loudly. Strange atmosphere in here tonight, I said to Carol, who replied with a knowing air, it's only 8, they just opened, what do you expect? I looked at the clock and saw that she was right. I sighed. At this time of night on a weekday, there were many places I should have been, but a bar wasn't one of them. A cold draught whipped through the door. I ordered a glass of wine without checking what Carol would like, downed it quickly and decided to stop asking myself what I wanted— not just today but in general. So, you came, said Carol, her fingers drumming a victory march on the wooden bar. In reply I said, you do know that Ines is in hospital because she had a hard time coping with that evening with you two? Did she? asked Carol and slid nearer to me. I found the greed on her face hard to stomach. Whenever she threw back her red mane, her perfume grew even more intense. She must have doused herself in it to mark the occasion. A short, blond guy in a worn-out denim suit was strutting about. The champagne was not a good idea—it was obvious that she didn't want to drink. Carol shook her head to express her concern and understanding, but only very slightly. It's a common, everyday situation. You can't protect her from it. I said nothing. And anyway, it was Rebecca who ordered the drinks, and she's not in the know, so how can you blame me? You don't even believe that yourself! I snorted, Rebecca knows *everything*. And she did it on purpose. And as her girlfriend . . . Carol suddenly let her head fall. What's the matter? I asked. It might not last much longer, she said, my relationship with Rebecca.

Her relationship with Rebecca—Jesus, as if I was really interested. I'd have one more glass of wine and then I'd be off. I gave the barkeeper a sign. I had to hand it to him—whatever else I didn't like about this bar, the staff worked like they'd been trained by Speedy Gonzales, or were on speed. I don't know, it's hard to explain, said Carol. She ruins everything. Not the way Ines ruins everything. Rebecca does it with a few words. When I light candles for dinner, she says I have a perverse romantic streak. Carol stared at the counter in front of her; not smoking or drinking, just talking, and I was moved by the way she took for granted that I was interested. I tried to imagine Carol and Rebecca having a candlelit dinner in their sterile flat, but it was impossible. At first I thought she was just jealous, continued Carol, but now I think she actually gets pleasure from that kind of thing. Then you should leave straight away, I replied. I'm starting to feel I should too, she answered. What does that mean—won't she let you? Now I wasn't being sympathetic—I was alarmed. No, I can't find a place. I gave a short laugh. The things I imagined. But her admission gave me great satisfaction and I watched the blond guy, who had started dancing, in a slightly better mood. He jerked his head from left to right with unnatural, choppy movements as if posing for mug shots. The way he danced, you'd think that joy was a ridiculous notion. Carol continued. First, I clung to the idea that it had been special for her. Yeah? I was only half-listening. The first time with a woman was like the first time ever for me. But it seems that it's not the same for everyone. For her, it was just a drunken mistake. A mistake that she kept making, just like she kept going on drinking binges. A total paradox—as if she could undo it all by doing it again and again. Perhaps she really tried to feel something, but she couldn't. Only now did it dawn on me that Carol was talking about Ines, not Rebecca. She was explaining it to me—but even if her account had been twice as convincing and she'd carried on till the small hours of the morning, I didn't want to know. And Kai? I interrupted. Didn't he notice anything? It's strange, Carol said. I saw him the other day in a gallery and I wanted to avoid him, but he came over to me, almost ran across the room in fact, and said: Carol, if you can make her happy then it's fine by me. I just want you to know that it's up to her. I won't fight for her. I've used up all my energy. I see, I said. What exhibition were you in? Sorry? asked Carol. What exhibition were you in when you met Kai? At the Schirn. Why? No reason. I made the barkeeper a sign for a refill. That doesn't solve anything, Carol said. I nodded. I didn't want to solve anything—I just wanted a drink. Kai, she said with some effort, her voice sounding strangled, Kai says that he drinks much more since he met her.

There was no way I wanted Carol to drive me home. I wanted to leave the same way I had come— proud, alone and by taxi. I went out onto the street and started looking around but there were none. Not wanting to go back in because of Carol, I decided to start walking towards home; one was bound to turn up. But no sooner had I walked a block than I realized that the fresh air was doing me good. I broadened my stride and buried my hands deep into my pockets. I tried hard to breathe in deeply and walk in a straight line. My cheeks were glowing. Lit-up shop windows slid past me; in a blur, I took in a bookshop, a shoe shop and a hairdresser's. I walked quickly, focussing all my concentration on my steps. I could have carried on for hours. By now it wasn't worth hailing a taxi even if one came. A taxiless city, I thought, sobering up slowly. Then, just as I was crossing a junction, I saw it—the enormous poster.

The oversized face. As if glued to the spot, I stood in the middle of the street and stared until a car honked me. There she was. 22D. Yoda. The party slogan was: *Forgetting doesn't count*, then her face, her familiar face. Her eyes were as big as dinner plates, the pores of her skin clearly visible, individual hairs, liver spots. But that wasn't what struck me. It was the name underneath her photo: Rebecca, 92. I didn't understand. Why Rebecca? I slowly surfaced from the watery depths of my mind like a deep-sea diver, broke through the surface and felt astonishingly clear. I put together the pieces of my consciousness: the old woman I had named Yoda was also called Rebecca. Or it was just the name given to her by the ad people. It was nothing more than a coincidence, but one that I intensely disliked. I trudged on. At the kiosk near Richard's flat, I bought an ice-cold Coke and knocked it back in one go. Afterwards, my throat and part of my stomach felt numb, but I felt sober. And now I was here, I could save myself the rest of the journey and stay the night at Richard's. It took me a while to find his doorbell. Richard greeted me through the intercom with wholehearted enthusiasm. I paused for a moment to put a chewing gum in my mouth, then the door buzzer went and I entered Richard's building, prolonging what had already been a hell of a long day.

Cautiously, as the lights still hadn't been repaired, I made my way upstairs to the top, using the dull glow from my mobile to light each step in front of me. The door was ajar. In the hallway, the digger wasn't where it was usually parked—in its place was a pair of tiny trainers. Richard called from his study: Just a minute, I'm on the phone. I hung up my scarf and parka, then looked into the kitchen. The plastic tablecloth was spread, on which Leonard's plate with the dwarves was laid, empty except for a few tomato stalks and a carefully bitten-off, oval bread crust. Leonard was sitting cross-legged on the carpeted floor in his bedroom, lit by the pleasant glow from his desk lamp whose long neck he had pulled down towards him. He was leafing through a picture book, already in his pyjamas but clearly wide awake. Next to him on the floor, rewrapped in their aluminium foil, lay several cracked, chocolate Kinder eggs. He had only been interested in what was inside them, and these now formed a proud row to guard his sleeping quarters: a pirate, Spiderman, a knight and a blue monster I didn't recognize.

Leonard and I stared at each other with intense scrutiny, engaged in a brief power struggle—my gaze was very tired, his very awake. Hi, he said after a while, without looking very surprised and I answered, hi Leonard and took a little step into his room. He had changed since the photo in the hallway was taken—his hair was short and not as curly, his face square and white. He was very stoutly built, resembling less a praline and more a little butcher boy. Hello, he greeted me, a complete stranger in his room, with the casual air only a child of divorce could muster, and, as he turned back to his book, I heard him murmur, Maya the Bee. I looked down at myself and saw that I had on a lemon-yellow-and-black outfit. I sat down next to him on the floor, crossing my legs with some effort. Seen from below, the room looked bigger. The light from the desk lamp shone on his empty bed; I eyed the mussed-up bedclothes in the twilight, which, in my state of exhaustion, looked exquisitely inviting. You're not asleep yet? I enquired. He was a polite boy; he didn't ignore my question, even if he might have found it superfluous. He looked at me, slight disconcertion in his large brown eyes. No, he said, the phone woke me up. Then he showed me his book and I realized he was asking me to read to him. I began right away, my intonation exaggerated; not knowing many children, I was quite nervous. I read until Leonard stretched out his feet, inside their red-and-blue checked, not very clean socks, and looked towards the door with a serious expression to where his father now stood, still holding the phone, probably having watched the scene for quite some time. Sorry, Richard said, waving the phone. He looked as tired as I felt and the way the three of us stood apart in the room, it was as if we formed a system of rotating planets, each dealing in their way with the conditions in their own world, and moving along completely separate orbits.

We put Leonard to bed, and the sight of him lying there made me terribly tired. I wrenched open my mouth but found I couldn't yawn. With the lights dimmed, a cognac glass in hand, Richard and I outdid each other in reporting the banalities of the day; but our behaviour only seemed so absurd because I was looking for signs that he'd sensed I'd been cheating on him. When he began stroking my hand, I awkwardly pulled it away. Hey, I said, changing the subject, I got a real shock on the way over here. Around the corner from here there's a billboard for that Eyewitnesses to History campaign—I'm sure you've already seen it? It's just an ad, but still. In any case, I came around the corner—and there was this face.

Richard, who had been looking intently at me, said: Interesting you should mention it, we're running that story in the paper on Monday. I set down the cognac glass I'd just picked up. What story? I asked. It seemed like a strange coincidence. Richard also set down his glass and said, Well, she's not a Jew . . . in fact, she's the widow of an SS Division Commander from Breslau who's now earning a tidy packet on the side by playing a Jew in this campaign and other bit parts on TV. I observed him the way he articulated his words, just like in those big editorial meetings— the political journalist from head to toe. I realized it wasn't just his sense of morality that made him want to run this story, no—this article would also damage the party that had commissioned this well-meaning campaign, and our paper was closer in sympathies to the opposition. Just business as usual, but this time it annoyed me and I resented him and his smug attitude. How can the old woman help that? I said. It's ridiculous, a completely pointless bit of scandal, and it's only because Blüher loves that kind of thing. Richard didn't like that—he didn't like to think he was doing something for the editor-in-chief's sake. He immediately flew off the handle. Well, she's getting good money for it, and her children—the offspring of an SS henchman—they're raking it in! Yes, I said, sure. But isn't it the photographer's look-out? No, said Richard, caught unawares, instantly switching to a tone of arrogance. The photographer just snapped the pictures, he doesn't have to report anything. I wanted to argue but I let it pass—or, rather, I grabbed my cognac glass and thought about my recent report on social-welfare families. In it, the kids weren't kids, the dirt wasn't dirt and the spider's webs weren't spider's webs. And the families, who we'd sat on their tattered sofas and talked to while we took their pictures, looked as if we had roughed them up in our contrived, ugly aesthetic, as if we'd creased their clothes and daubed them with mustard and ketchup, as if we'd placed some ripped magazines next to the remote control in the living room before we described the scene or pressed the shutter. *Not real*. And as we made notes and took photographs, we didn't know whether we were behaving outrageously or were just helpless. We escaped into delusions of grandeur and snobbish posturing that this was how we could *make a difference*. That photo will be a big opener, it's very good, said Richard, who was embarrassed by his outburst, and I nodded. Why was he making it so easy for me? We finished our cognac in silence; I turned off the light. Come here, he said and pulled me towards him. Despite our complete exhaustion, we both thought it was a good idea to sleep together to cast aside any misunderstandings and it felt good to lose myself in those familiar motions. But then, as I gently wound my legs around him, I began to think that our coupling, here in the illusory safety of the night, did not spring from passion but from the desire to forget—just as Ines had at some point started to drink, not from the desire to drink but to forget. And I regretted the fact that our act that night could be nothing more than a shallow compromise, a poor substitute; we hadn't found the right words. But even though love wasn't easy, at least we could say we had tried our very best.

I saw the red figures on the digital clock. 05:23. Although I was wide awake, I didn't stir. I wanted to stay there in the dark for as long as possible, watch the blackness around me turn to grey and enjoy the soft transition from night to day. When daylight came and our contours became visible, our problems would also take on a more solid form. And I watched the rising sun like an enemy claiming victory over this room and its inhabitants, making it lighter, nuance by nuance; an enemy that always managed to surprise me with its extraordinary beauty. This time—the way the sunrays filtered through the filaments of the curtains, the way they took on colour and dotted the room with small, bright patterns that splashed across the carpet, sliding up the lower bed-covers, all the way to us—was no exception. The duvet and my calves were speckled with irregular patterns like the fur of some exotic animal.

Richard was asleep in his corner of his bed, tightly wrapped in his cover and lying on his back, his preferred way of sleeping. And I couldn't help it— I had to touch the white cover, stroke it gently until the landscape changed and somewhere around the middle of his body an interesting little hillock formed. I was seized with tenderness, and caressed the small tent. All I needed was to carry on a little longer and he would bare himself, still half-asleep, and pull me close. I stood up quietly and took my clothes from the chair. Richard turned towards the wall, murmuring. He was used to me getting up early; I went swimming, he knew that. I looked at him and kissed him on the forehead. I wasn't really leaving him because we'd never really been together. Rather, it was as if we had sat together for a while on a park bench and had enjoyed the nice view. And I just happened to be the first one to get up and leave.

Over the next few days, I didn't see Richard or Kai or Ines. In the evenings, the phone rang and I knew that someone was listening to Susan's voice; but I didn't pick up and no one left a message. Exhausted by the complexity of the situation, I was not capable of experiencing or causing any more reactions. I braced myself in the attitude that things would sort themselves out if I kept very still; I wrapped myself in optimism—an optimism that flew in the face of how these kinds of situations normally turn out. What could happen, after all, except that time would bury all these fears and jealousies, all those deadly trenches in people's minds? Although Richard cooled off towards me at the office after he realized I was making excuses, and Kai, in his beautiful voice that made everyday words warmer and softer, made many promises, only to leave for a job in Hamburg, I had made my decision. It was a decision for a life with Kai and Ines, whatever that might be. I started to trust in fate, thought *things will be all right*, stifling my secret doubts that, by nurturing these confused fantasies, I was behaving like a rabbit on the motorway that thinks it sees the rising sun in the headlights of a lorry.

I visited Ines again; she let me know—a revelation that she didn't even have to put into words—that Carol was now an obliging delivery girl, and so I no longer felt I had to visit her every other day. And anyway, she would soon be discharged. Kai's not around, she murmured, and I reacted to this news with a stoic expression. Will you take me to the clinic? Yes, I said, I'll have to borrow a car, but that shouldn't be a problem. People had come into my life, and no matter whether I did them right or wrong, or vice versa, we had become close. It put me in a ridiculously good mood when I realized this; in fact, I was on the verge of hysteria, having not slept for days.

That evening after work, I walked the streets. The days were gradually getting longer, and, for the first time that afternoon, the spring sun had come out; it had driven people onto the streets and even now, at around half past eight in the evening when it was dark and the shops were closed, people teemed restlessly like ants and there were more cars and bikes about than usual. I had packed my court shoes in my bag and was wearing trainers; I took a detour, so as not to pass Richard's place, to the billboard where I had seen the portrait for the first time. Only a couple of days after the article had been printed, the poster had disappeared. Not even torn scraps of paper showed where it had been; Yoda's portrait hadn't been ripped down, it had been pasted over. I stood on the street for a while with my head leant back, looking up at the building, my hands thrust into the pockets of my coat, looking at the young woman in her underwear who'd replaced her; then I strolled on, my work bag slung over my shoulder, slowing down because I had nothing else to do. By then, I was in Bornheim, walking down never-ending Sandweg. On the other side of the street, I saw the illuminated window of a video-rental shop with two long glass facades, the right-hand one fixed with a sign: *Admission for over-18s only*. I spontaneously decided to become a member and went into the shop, or, more precisely, the adult section, and said good evening, which didn't raise the slightest interest from the only employee in the shop—a fifty-something, scruffily dressed man in a baseball cap, who was staring at the CCTV screen from behind his small counter. I stood at the counter and looked at the screen as well—nothing but empty corridors. It took me a while to spot a tall man in a checked shirt, who was wandering indecisively up and down the aisles. A sudden inspiration made me ask the man in the cap if they stocked Rebecca's film. I had to spell her long surname twice and he looked for a while on the computer but there was no entry. He said he was very sorry but I didn't mind that much. I wasn't so sure, after all, that I wanted to see a film by Rebecca that evening; perhaps another time. My inquiry about an unknown director had elevated me to the status of a film buff in the man's eyes and he very courteously issued me a membership card. He kept my ID to copy down my details, and I looked around while my card was being made. I strolled about the shelves of erotica for a while, looking more closely here and there at covers with titles such as *Teenage Vulvas* and *Big Lips*. There was that kind of stuff, of course, but also fairy-tale titles like *The Giant Hammer* or *Palace of Tits*, and I finally came to where erotica segued good-naturedly into horror. I chose a 1930s classic and then was keen to leave the place. Costs a euro for every calendar day started, said the man behind the counter, after handing me my laminated card.

At home I slipped off my coat and shoes, fetched myself an enormous glass of orange juice and started the film. It was about a circus full of mutants and freaks; in the shop, I'd read on the back cover that the film had been shot using actors with real deformities and I couldn't get this out of my mind as I watched the living, snake-like torso creeping along the ground who could light himself a cigarette by coordinating his lip movements. Or the men with tiny pinheads. Or the Siamese twins who, despite being physically joined, had married different men and sometimes argued about their schedules and daily routines. The story was about the Lilliputian Hans who, although happily engaged to a Lilliputian girl, is drawn to a beautiful trapeze artist, a conventionally attractive woman. She eventually marries Hans for his riches and fools him. A terrible wedding party ensues during which the Lilliputian girl, who is in love with him, and the audience, suffer with Hans. I was freezing. Sitting on the sofa with my knees up, my arms wrapped around my calves to make myself very small, I watched.

After half an hour, the film was nearly over when I thought I heard a solid smacking noise and automatically turned towards the window; it was exactly how the first bird had sounded when it flew against the window. I pressed the remote to pause the film and looked hesitantly at the closed curtain. Everything was quiet, almost eerily quiet. It took a while before I dared looked behind the curtain but I couldn't see a bird, not even when I went out onto the balcony. Nothing. Just the black, stiff branches of the chestnut tree in the backyard that normally withstood the rain but were now swaying in the wind of a brewing spring storm and looked like a Japanese paper cut-out that had been set a-dancing. Relieved, I went back into the living room. Before I let the film run on, I turned up the heating as I was suddenly cold. I looked at the closing credits, the penetrating tune in my ear and the lyrics: *One of us*. The revenge of the mutants was ghastly. In the end, the trapeze artist and her lover are deformed beyond recognition, writhing on the ground like worms; but here at least, inner values were reflected on the outside. The good guys had won, no matter if they were unsightly. And yet I had no feeling of satisfaction. Why had I rented a horror film anyway? I wandered through the flat for no particular reason, then I fished a map of the region out of my shoulder bag that I'd taken from the office.

The route into the Taunus looked pretty. You took the A66 from Frankfurt, then drove along the Rhine down Uferstrasse, overlooking the scenic vineyards around Eltville, the Town of Roses, before turning off into the countryside. After a gradually winding country road up the slopes, you soon arrived in the district of Schlangenbad where the clinic was. It wouldn't be a problem; you could hardly miss it. Roughly an hour, I guessed. And with my thoughts on this, I folded up the map again.

I had been swimming that morning and that night, I swam a second time. At first I didn't recognize it; the water was black—the kind of black which contains all the colours but which swallows them all. It had the alienating beauty of an installation but I didn't feel nearly as safe as in a museum. The logic of my dream sputtered: I swam towards the water, not with flowing but with staccato movements. It suddenly narrowed and turned into the black River Main. In the water, something white gleamed—the neck of a swan or the hand of someone drowning. I woke up— the room was icy cold. My night swim had been more exhausting than my morning one.

I picked up Ines in the car that I'd borrowed from an eager intern at the office, a dented Opel which had a collection of Coke cans, pizza boxes and old newspapers. I also found a CD set of *The Magic Flute*. The interior of the car smelt slightly of pine needles which I traced back to the little pine-tree air freshener that was swaying from the ceiling in the front. I had misgivings about the car but it started with no problem. When Ines came out of the front door in an unzipped orange ski jacket, wearing a blazer and pullover underneath like an armoured animal, she didn't notice the car. She was swinging a sports bag and, as she opened the passenger door, she dropped her barely smoked cigarette on the ground. She leant over the gearstick with her free hand to hug me. I could smell her breakfast-time whisky. Get in, I said, so she tried to slam the car door, almost leaving her sports bag on the pavement. Only when the door jammed did she notice and leant out. I started up the Opel and, with the pine tree swinging to the overture of Mozart's opera, we drove off.

I cruised at a steady speed after we left the city; there wasn't much traffic. Soon the Rhine glittered to our left, and now and again, a ship sounded its horn. All the way to the Taunus, Ines didn't say a word. She had wound down the window and put on a pair of sunglasses; and the way she was playing with the pine tree by tapping it and making it swing, while singing Papageno's part in a soft soprano as clear as a bell, she was beginning to look more and more like a keyed-up skier going on holiday.

The woods we drove through had seemed lifeless from a distance—a dark-green patch in the landscape: but as we entered them, they changed. The morning fog had dispersed and now we crossed a green backdrop bathed in early-morning sunshine. Ines stretched her arm out of the open window; birds twittered and slowly, everything took on colour, indicating trees and bushes, even the odd warning sign of wild animals. We left the foothills behind and now, in place of the pine trees, the landscape gave way to meadows, bordered by a sea of leafy birches and interspersed with variegated bushes and soft brushwood. Here and there, fallen trees could be seen, some lying crossways on the ground, roots stuck up in the air, upended by the recent storms. It was as if we were leaving the real world and entering a fairy tale. Ines, who had stopped singing by now and was staring, mesmerized, out of the window, took the occasional sip from her hip flask and said: A nice spot, very nice, let's stop and take a little walk.

I turned onto the next dirt track and turned off the engine. Ines was looking for something in her anorak pocket, her forehead wrinkled in concentration, as if she were gathering her strength for a difficult step, and I was secretly afraid that she'd guessed everything and would now confront me. She suddenly seemed very distant, and I wasn't sure if I'd made a mistake by driving her out here. But then she found what she was looking for: another hip flask, which she stuck into her ski jacket before opening the car door with a relaxed, peaceful expression. Aren't you too hot in all those jackets, I asked her, but she had already set off, walking down the dirt track at a fast pace, and didn't answer. I followed her garish orange trainers, cautiously setting one foot in front of the other and carefully holding up my long coat; my God, I was dressed completely inappropriately for a walk in the woods. I'd have liked to have called after her, saying that I hadn't realized that 'taking a little walk' meant going on a hike; at the same time, I didn't want to hold her back. It was an important day for her and we had plenty of time. But the woods that had seemed so tempting from the car seemed more and more threatening to me; the soft, snapping sounds that I caused with each step despite being careful made me realize that I was an alien element, helplessly at the mercy of my surroundings. Beyond a curve in the path, past which I'd guessed there was a clearing, was just more woodland; as soon as I thought the woods would get denser, we arrived in a bright area overgrown with bushes. I didn't understand the system here. It was an unusually mild day after the storms and thunder of the past few nights; the woods were breathing and cracking, and I was sure that, at any moment, a living creature would peer out from behind a tree—human or animal. But no one showed up; on the contrary—after the next bend, Ines disappeared. I grew worried yet forced myself not to run after her, not to panic. Just a few brave yards further and she'd appear again. It was suddenly alarmingly quiet; the sound of the wind was swallowed by the thicket and when I looked up, there was no sky, only green. Here and there, an excited little bird appeared and cut through the air with jerky, shrill sounds; but as soon as it disappeared, the silence blanketed everything again like cotton wool, muffling all sound; and my steps, their crunching and cracking sounds, seemed infinitely loud. A stick fell down noisily to the ground next to me, probably dropped by a daredevil bird. I felt attacked.

Slowly my eyes began to get used to the colours, began to differentiate between browns and greys, and it was as if I had gained a new sense; I wondered whether Ines, the painter, also saw this palette full of nuances, wherever she was. I also got used to hiking in my shoes by only treading on the balls of my feet; it was more tiring but also more efficient. Ines, I cried out quietly, almost inaudibly, Ines, it's about time now. I wasn't even sure whether I was going in the right direction. The wood was getting denser and tears sprang to my eyes. What if she vanished in this damn wood, never to be seen again? Perhaps she had only lured me here to be a witness. But then I came to a clearing and saw her: her neon clothing glowed and she was sitting on a stone, bent forward slightly, one hand pressed to her chest, the other hanging down at her side. She looked like a large, orange-coloured troll, so sunken in thought that I didn't want to disturb her. I just stood there by the bush and gazed at her. I thought: perhaps trolls had sprung up because Adam and Eve had produced so many children that they were embarrassed and hid some in caves, so that God wouldn't notice. And these children lived underground in shame for so long that they transformed into these hybrid creatures. I waited until she saw me, but she took no notice although she certainly knew I was standing just a few yards from her; then she drank a little sip from the hip flask. Now and again, she sprinkled the moss with some drops, then drank again, laughing as she did so. The light formed a halo around her, bathing her anorak in a silver lustre. My heart beat fast and I felt my cheeks flush. Right now, I thought, she's not ashamed, but I am unspeakably ashamed—for her and the whole world. Ines, I called, quietly, as I slowly approached her, calling her name over and over again in a soothing way until she lifted her head.

Until I was a yard from her, I hadn't realized that she was crying. Now I saw it; now I understood the delay as I took in the details: her hanging shoulders, her twisted mouth, her shiny cheeks, radiant in a way that looked as if they were light itself. I hesitated, then stopped, and here, faced with my crying sister, my thoughts took me far away from these woods to that sea resort where our parents had taken a photo of Ines laughing while I buried her in the sand. It had been twenty years earlier, not so long ago. And in this magical forest under radiant trees whose leaves seemed to give light instead of shade, it felt as if it had only been yesterday since everything had changed so much; in fact, it seemed quite possible that right here, right now, everything could change again and we, Ines and I, could somehow straighten out our lives, behind which something like happiness, as a system of coordinates, would shine through, a junction of events, thoughts and relations which we would always be able to fall back on; and I believed it right then—for some reason, I believed it. I stood motionless in those sunlit woods. I watched Ines put aside her hip flask and draw a line in the moss with a thin stick, and I abandoned myself to the absurd hope flooding through me that these woods might prevent any harm coming to us—here, now—that they could shield us with protective magic, a magic that was no less than an unspoken, unspeakable gift, handed to us by life when it gave us souls ruled by tenderness and patience, so that our lives would finally come in line with the vision of the good life we carried inside and kept catching glimpses of, even if only as shadows that turned the corner a couple of paces ahead—as a sign and allusion, as a road leading up a hill, beyond which lay another hill and which, when you'd crossed it, always showed a view across new hills, with an ever-wilder, more tempting, endless

landscape, a landscape in which we would eventually
find settlements, houses that we would be beckoned
into, doors that opened, only to reveal more doors,
an endless folly that we would be subject to—and
above us, the deceptive sky, so blue it might make
you sick, a sky in Technicolor. A finch suddenly flitted
up into the air, plunged after a few yards and recon-
quered the air as if it were a mechanical toy. The
world is so colourful, said Ines dreamily, looking
down at the earth. All the colours put together pro-
duce something like dirt. Then she threw away the
stick and abruptly stood up. Let's go, she said.

Ten minutes later we had arrived at the large
entrance. I drove slowly up the gravel path. As we
came nearer, we saw a few people standing next to
the imposing building, smoking and talking. All of a
sudden, Ines was in a hurry to belong to this group—
or at least that was how it seemed to me. She quickly
said goodbye; I now realized that I wasn't at all ready
for her to leave. I gazed after her as she walked with
that brisk, even step—except for her slight limp—
that people have when there is a goal in sight. She
swung her sports bag and then, before she rang the
bell and the door opened, she turned to wave to me
from the last few yards. Then the door opened and
she crossed the threshold to the clinic as if it were the
finishing line. I remained seated in the car. The hours
ran into each other, the sun gave out. Twilight took

over the surroundings. I smoked and waited for something to happen—for Ines to come running back out, or something like that. But nothing of the sort happened. The lights came on in the building. The trees swayed gently in the wind, otherwise all was quiet. No one came or went from the clinic; my mobile rang three times, then everything was silent again. Eventually the door opened and I was almost relieved; I was convinced it would be Ines. Instead, it was a woman with a small girl who was hugging an enormous teddy to her chest. The mother looked tearful, the girl happy, perhaps because she had seen her father. I would have liked nothing more than to run over to the mother and ask what she thought of the clinic, how often she was allowed to visit, how things developed after someone went through that door; but they had already disappeared into their car, the child was fastened in the back with a seatbelt and I saw her wave to me, so full of trust, smiling through the window in my direction.